Praise for To

The Man Who Fell

"Dazzlingly accomplished." —*Post Book World*

"The miracle of this novel is that it obliges us to rethink our whole idea of narration and history and myth. Tom Spanbauer takes us into territories where few of us would ever dare to go."
—*New York Times Book Review*

"A novel of enormous imaginative scope....*The Man Who Fell in Love with the Moon* is a perceptive, moving story that begs to be read, not just once but again and again."
—*Washington Blade*

"A wise and wonderful tale. *The Man Who Fell in Love with the Moon* is a beautifully conceived, warm and generous novel with the power to work some deep magic, to heal and to transport."
—*Miami Herald*

"A haunting, earthy, and deeply felt tale of love and loss."
—*Publishers Weekly*

"A masterful plot....Delightfully unpredictable and compelling."
—*Library Journal*

"Every once in a while a reviewer comes across a book that seems so startlingly original and true that it redeems everything: art, life, the human spirit, a reviewer's job....Tom Spanbauer's novel *The Man Who Fell in Love with the Moon* is such a book."
—*Willamette Week*, Oregon

ALSO BY TOM SPANBAUER

The Man Who Fell in Love with the Moon

FARAWAY PLACES

Tom Spanbauer

Grateful acknowledgment is made for permission to reprint excerpts from the following copyrighted material:

"Dark Town Strutter's Ball" by S. Brooks copyright © 1917 renewed 1945 Leo Feist, Inc. All rights assigned to SBK Catalogue Partnership. All rights controlled and administered by SBK Feist Catalog. International copyright secured. Made in USA. All rights reserved. Used by permission.

"Sixteen Tons" by Merle Travis copyright © 1947 by American Music, Inc. Copyright renewed and assigned to Elvis Presley Music and Unichappell Music, Inc. All rights administered by Unichappell Music, Inc. International copyright secured. All rights reserved. Used by permission.

A hardcover edition of this book was published in 1988 by G. P. Putnam's Sons. It is here reprinted by arrangement with G. P. Putnam's Sons.

HarperCollins books may be purchased for educational, business, or sales promotional use. For information please write: Special Markets Department, HarperCollins Publishers, Inc., 10 East 53rd Street, New York, NY 10022.

First HarperPerennial edition published 1993.

Library of Congress Cataloging-in-Publication Data

Spanbauer, Tom.
Faraway places / Tom Spanbauer. — 1st HarperPerennial ed.
p. cm.
ISBN 0-06-097552-0 (pbk.)
I. Title
[PS3569.P339F37] 1993
813′.54—dc20 92-54844

---

93 94 95 96 97 CW 10 9 8 7 6 5 4 3 2 1

My thanks to J.D. Dolan,
Stacy Creamer, and Eric Ashworth;
also, to Ellie Covan and the Dixon
Placemats.

To Clyde Hall:
Un son baisch

The moon was full and it was the February that it didn't snow. I had my flannel pajamas on and my loafer socks, and I was in the bathroom looking into the mirror watching myself brush my teeth after *One Man's Family* on the radio but before the rosary, when my mother walked through the hallway with the wallpaper that had the butterflies and the dice on it. She went past the bathroom door in her green kimono with that look on her face, her left eye cockeyed. I spit—the white toothpaste turned pink with my blood—then rinsed my mouth and the sink. By the time I got to the kitchen I could feel it too.

The kitchen door was open and so was the screen. The screen door's spring had been disconnected for winter and without that spring to snug it back into home, the door drifted between open and closed, lost on its hinges. My mother was standing out by the gate by the time I got to the kitchen. That gate was unlatched and drifting too, like the screen door. My mother's hair blew back off her face. She'd stood herself into the wind—wind that was blowing from a direction it had never blown from before. And the wind was warm, which was something new—something it had never been. Not in February.

"Chinook," my mother said softly, almost so soft I couldn't hear, and then she crossed herself. "Chinook," she said again, this time loud enough for the sky and moon. She said the word this second time as if calling out to some long-lost friend whose name she had forgotten, then suddenly remembered. But the chinook was no friend; it was the name for the strange wind blowing. And by November, everything that had been stirred up and blown around by that chinook since February was all settled back down again. And all was finished up.

But nothing was ever the same.

That woman Sugar Babe was dead, and Harold P. Endicott was dead next, and then the nigger was dead. Always in threes, death, my mother would say, then cross herself. Between the drought and that year of the chinook, by November we were all finished up too—let go of, unlatched. The house got burned down, and the barn too, along with the toolshed and most of our stuff, and we lost the farm for good.

The chinook lasted all the next day and night until the morning after. When I got up that third day, my mother looked like her old self again. The whole time that the chinook blew on us my mother was a mess. That's what my father said to her, *You're a mess,* he said, because she couldn't cook normal. My father's eggs were hard and his mush was burnt and we had tuna casserole for supper when it wasn't even Friday. That whole chinook time my mother didn't put her hair up in the day and comb it out for my father at suppertime or put lipstick on or wear her clean apron over her red housedress when it came time to get things done. Besides the cooking, my father said my mother was a mess because she had just let herself go. *Mom,* my father said to her, *just take a good look at yourself. You're just letting yourself go.*

Hawks blew in the second morning of the chinook

and perched in the poplars in front of our house. My mother watched them from the front window—crossing herself and watching them the whole day. That night we prayed the rosary, her mixing up the sorrowful mysteries with the glorious ones, eyes still on the poplars, though you couldn't make out a single bird or branch past dark.

The following morning the hawks were gone, my mother was back, normal, getting the eggs right and roast beef for supper. But those hawks showed up again, not in the poplars in front of the house, but in the stand of cottonwood trees up the river—not that I said anything to my mother about the hawks showing up there.

The red flags that hung on the fence were made out of old flour sacks cut into triangle shapes and dyed in Rit by my mother. My father hung the red flags from the barbed wire, one every mile for the four miles that our road traveled to the main road to town. My mother and my father did that with the red flags long before the chinook. In fact, those red flags hung there on that fence maybe even before I was around. I never asked, but I don't ever remember the red flags not hanging there marking the distance.

At the second flag you came to, there were three miles left before you got to the house, and right there, at the second red flag, the ground went down. On that slope you could see on both sides of you for just about forever. It was a plateau caused by the river going down slowly over the centuries to the place where it is now, the Portneuf River—a river, at its widest, no wider than double the width of the main road to town.

Standing there at the second flag and looking down onto the valley, you felt like you were standing on the world and the world was in endless space, which is the case—I know—but standing there you really got the sense that you were standing on a round ball. You had to lean back to keep your balance, to keep from falling forward and off. Either that or you got the feeling that the world was as flat as a cookie sheet with a ripple in it and the sky was just a big dome. At night God punched holes in the dome with a needle that were stars. But in either case, whether you were leaning back so as not to fall off the ball, or if you were lying flat on the cookie sheet with the ripple in it under the big dome, whatever, the sky was the thing; the unstoppable sky was the thing.

There was sky everywhere: outside the windows, under the beds, between the ceiling and the floor there was sky. There was sky between your fingers when you spread them, and sky under your arms when you lifted them up. Sky around your neck and ears and head, and sky pressing against your eyeballs. When you took a breath you were breathing sky. Sky was in your lungs. My mother hung up wash across the sky. I swung in my swing through the sky. There was no escaping it. The sky was as everywhere as the nuns at the St. Joseph's School said God was. Only the ground stopped it, and even then it didn't stop there. It was all an illusion, like Mr. Energy, that magician at the Blackfoot State Fair, said. Everything was an illusion according to him. I used to get scared at night just thinking about it: what if everything—everything that was familiar to me, everything I knew—was an illusion and what I was really doing was hanging in thin air, like the earth was hanging in thin air, like I could see the moon hanging up there in the sky, a round ball just out there with nothing solid to hold it in place.

Besides the sky and the graveled road and the fence with the red triangles hanging on it, and the power lines, and the fence on the other side of the road, this is what you could see from the second flag up there on the plateau: you could see the road, straight as an arrow. Mormons built that road, which is the only thing Mormons are good at besides having kids, my mother would say, crossing herself: making things straight. That road went straight to the river, but never crossed it because Matisse County was low on funds for a bridge. The fences on both sides of the road were just as straight as the road. Mormons built them too, I figured. On the other side of the fences, there was barley planted, or sugar beets, or spuds, or alfalfa, depending on the rotation. But it was always green, on the other side of the fences—in the spring, that is—

and after that things got gold and brown, but mostly brown, and especially that year.

You could see our house sticking up out of the world like the tip of a sword that pierced the round ball and stuck out just that far on the other side. You could see the barn too, broad and tall. Looked more like a castle to me, brick, and heavy, not like the sky.

You could see the toolshed. In the sun, the tin square toolshed with its sloping roof was so bright you couldn't look at it. Sometimes I used to think that the toolshed in the sun—sky all around it—was like God. You couldn't bear to look. And even if you could, you couldn't see. And that long, cool rectangle of shade from the barn was Jesus. By the end of the day, Jesus always cooled down God enough so you could look at Him. Sometimes the toolshed was Communism and the shadow of the barn creeping toward it was America. And sometimes the toolshed was the Mormons and the shadow of the barn was Catholicism. Sometimes the toolshed was my father, and my mother the shadow.

You could see the river from up there on the plateau. Well, not the river exactly, but the trees that lined the river. Out there on the cookie sheet, trees only grew along the river, except for the four poplars in front of our house. At one time there was a fifth, but lightning got to it. You could also see the stand of cottonwood trees up there where the river dog-legs, all twenty-two of them. You could see the catalpa tree that stuck up alone on the other side of the river, upriver about a quarter-mile from the stand of cottonwoods; and under that catalpa tree, you could barely make out the lean-to where the Indian woman, Sugar Babe, lived with the nigger. Then, to the southeast, downstream and across the river, you could see that big bunch of trees that I never counted, where Harold P. Endicott lived in his big stone house with his five dogs, Dobermans. Hellhounds, my mother called them, and crossed herself when she called them that.

You couldn't really see the big stone house for all the trees, but you could always see Harold P. Endicott's big American flag snapping in the wind up there in the sky.

You could see the road start up again on the other side of the river, beyond the trees, and keep going and going until the sky got to it.

And that's it. You could see the Oldsmobile maybe, and maybe sometimes my mother or my father walking across the yard, but most of the time you just thought you could see them, when really you couldn't at all.

Of course, when you got closer, say, between the last of the red flags and the house, you could see the Virginia creeper on the side of the house, and the horses and the holsteins in the corral, and the gas pump, and the lawn by the back porch with the fence around it, and my father's chair on the front porch, and the picnic table, and in the yard the machinery parked around:

the tractor, the plow, the disc, the harrow, and all those things, all of them John Deere.

And the most remarkable thing: the closer you got to the house, the more you could hear, and generally the hearing didn't catch up with the doing, so my mother could walk out the kitchen door, and that spring—when it was hooked up right—would slam the screen door back into home, but my mother would be on her second step out of there before the slam got to you.

I didn't like to think about that slam too much because it was more proof of that illusion stuff, or else that my ears were slower than my eyes. I couldn't decide which, but I already had more than my share of things not making any sense; I figured I wouldn't dwell on troubling matters anymore than was necessary.

At sunset sometimes I used to like to go out on the road in front of the house, under the poplars, and sit so that the sun looked like it was going down right in line with the road. I wondered if you could ever fly a plane fast enough into the sun so that it was always sunset. Or maybe you could shoot an arrow as big as an electric pole right at the sun. You could sit on the electric pole and hang on tight, flying right into the big red ball, going fast enough to stay ahead of any sound, silently headed for bull's-eye.

We never said much, my mother, my father, and me, when we drove to Mass in the Oldsmobile on Sunday morning. My mother didn't allow the radio—said it was a time for reflection—so we were all quiet and examined our consciences for sins, which I was getting to have a lot of—one particular mortal kind especially. My father drove—he was always the one who drove—and we reflected, me in the back seat, like always, looking out at the red flags, counting them like mortal sins to the main road, and then on the main road the fifteen miles or so to Wind River and then to the St. Joseph's Church for nine-o'clock Mass that we always got to at eight-thirty so we could make it to confession.

On the way home it was different, but not a lot; still no radio. We still didn't talk much, but we weren't reflecting anymore. We were in the State of Grace. We always stopped at the Wyz-Way market, where my mother bought groceries and my father smoked Viceroys and talked business with the other Catholic men whose wives were buying groceries too. I usually read comics and had a Snickers candy bar and a Coke. Actually, that is what I used to do, before that year: read comics. I was still having Snickers and Cokes like other years, but that year I was reading other things at the magazine stand.

There was one Sunday in particular I recall. It was just before Easter. I'd given up Snickers for Lent that year, so I was only drinking Coke. The day was sunny and cold. I was wearing my blue parka—my winter coat that year—and two pairs of socks along with long johns that were getting too short. Those long johns wouldn't stay stuck in my socks even when I wore two pairs. They'd slowly ride up, making big lumps where there weren't supposed to be any, especially on Sunday. I was catching up on what interested me most. The only woman in Elvis Presley's life was his mother; and Montgomery Clift had a secret death wish, though I never got to find out why Montgomery Clift wanted to die so bad. My father told me to stop filling my head with that movie-star crap and get in the car.

That was the Sunday, too, that we drove home a different way. I forget for what reason; I think my mother just wanted to try something new, so we drove across town, under the viaduct. When you drove that way, you had to drive past West Center and First Street by the railroad tracks, the warehouses, the St. Anthony's Hospital, Niggertown—five or six houses all clumped together—and the bars. It was there that we saw that woman's car, Sugar Babe's blue '49 Ford, sitting in front of a cinder-block building with a garbage can knocked over and garbage all over in front of it. There was a neon sign that said "WORKING MAN'S CLUB" in pink letters with a blue neon half-moon rising above in the window. We stared at the car and at the neon sign and the garbage all over and my mother crossed herself. I imagined Montgomery Clift in there drinking martinis in that special kind of glass, just wanting to die, and some guy from one of those houses in Niggertown playing a saxophone.

"That's her car, all right." my father said. "That woman Sugar Babe's."

My father slowed down the Oldsmobile. My mother moved closer to the window and so did I.

"Pat Mulekey back at the Wyz-Way was just saying today that's where that woman works," my father said. "Waitressing."

"Isn't she an Indian?" my mother said.

"Full-blood Sho-Ban," my father said. "Daughter of one of them old True Shots out there. Straight off the reservation."

"Forevermore!" my mother said, which was something my mother always said.

"Doesn't figure!" my father said. "Those Injuns out there don't like niggers no more than we do, and there she is, a full-blood, waitressing in that place. And living with one of them, too, out there in that lean-to!"

"Shh!" my mother said, and pointed to the back seat with her head.

"Means trouble! But those kind of people just got a nose for it," my father said.

This is what my room looked like: the wallpaper was brown with big green leaves on it and bluebirds flying.

It was upstairs, the only room there was upstairs. It was the attic. My window looked out onto the yard. In winter my father put plastic on the window so when you looked out it was like looking through someone's glasses who was nearsighted. In the mornings in winter the sun coming in the window made it glow orange.

There was my single bed with a green bedspread, the chest of drawers, the nightstand with a lamp on it that looked like a wagon wheel, with cowboys on the lampshade. There was a statue of St. Joseph that glowed in the dark. The door to the closet slanted with the roof and on the floor was linoleum that looked like somebody had spilled raisins all over it, and there was a green throw rug on the floor by the bed.

The only other thing in the room was a picture of a guardian angel helping two kids across a bridge. When I got confirmed I put my Holy Confirmation certificate on the wall next to the picture, so there was that too.

There were thirteen steps up to my room from the hallway that had the wallpaper with the butterflies and the dice. I always counted the steps when I went up and when I went down.

There were sixteen steps up to the loft of the barn. Whenever you walked up those stairs you heard the sound that the pigeons made with their wings. It didn't matter how quiet you went up there, you always scared the pigeons enough to get them flapping. They would fly through the loft till their wings made waves in the dust they had stirred up. You could see those waves in the light that bored down through the holes in the roof.

There were two windows up there in the barn's loft, one at either end, set in the triangles cut by the roof. They were big windows—big enough to get the hay through—though we'd stopped stacking hay up there long ago. The wood had gotten too old; the floorboards were rotten. In some places you couldn't even walk anymore, let alone stack hay. The front window was always closed, its swinging doors nailed shut, but the back window was perpetually open: the doors to it had fallen completely off. We used them as wood panels for the pig pen.

The back window of the barn was like another window: the rose window in the St. Joseph's Church in town, which was in the back too, in the choir loft. On Sunday at eight-thirty when you were standing there in line waiting for confession, reflecting and examining your conscience, somebody up there in the choir loft would turn the electric organ on. The sound of that organ starting up was like the sound the pigeons made when they flew through the light coming down from the holes in the roof.

The rose window in the St. Joseph's Church, which was mostly blue, presented a picture of the Holy Pentecost, which is when the Holy Ghost came down onto the apostles in the form of tongues of fire over their heads, even over Jesus'. The Holy Ghost, in the shape of a dove, appeared high above their haloed and inflamed heads. I figured the sound He made that Pentecost Sunday was just like the sound of the electric organ turning on, or like the sound the pigeons made once you got them going. It was the same sound the crows were making that night that I found the nigger hanging there.

From out the back window of the barn you could see how the roof jutted out in a V shape, and under the eave there the winch was attached, the winch we used to haul heavy things up with a rope, and then from the winch two tracks of flat iron went right down the middle of the barn lengthwise, under the ridgepole, from one end of the barn to the other, from one window to the other. It was broke too. No way you could slide anything down those tracks. All they were good for was the pigeons sitting on them. And of course, those tracks were covered with crusty piles of pigeon crap, and the floor too, in some places up to your ankles. It was that high. When the pigeons were sitting up there or when they were flying out, you had to be careful that they didn't crap on you, even though my mother said that her mother, Grandma Hannah, always said that it was good luck when a bird—a dove or a pigeon, or even better, a crow—singled you out that way.

From the back window of the barn you could see the swing hanging from the biggest limb of the biggest cottonwood in the stand. To get to that swing in the cottonwood trees, you had to go through the gate at the back of the corral behind the barn. That's where the haystack was, fenced in by snow fence. The dirt road that went by the corral and the haystack pretty much followed the river up to the cottonwoods. I liked to take my boots off and walk on that powdery dirt barefoot with the river on one side of me and the field of alfalfa on the other.

That place up there in the stand of twenty-two cottonwood trees smelled like the wind—a hot smell full of dry June grass and sagebrush and big round crusty cow pies and horse turds all mixed. It smelled like the river up there too—cool and shady and wet—making the air soft when you breathed in, and that summer, when the river went down and kept on going down to almost nothing, it was strong with dead fish—trout and suckers.

Under those trees that sound that the leaves made made you feel like you were having secrets whispered to you, and I whispered secrets back—like my secret name that I only said aloud there.

The sound of the leaves made you feel safe; a bunch of sticks shaking together—the sound gravel makes when you let the rocks pour out of your hand into the river. It was the only place around besides the loft in the barn where the sky got stopped some. In the barn you knew the sky was all around outside there, but as long as you were inside, in the loft, the high roof made you feel covered up from infinity. Under the cottonwood trees it wasn't quite so covered up as in the loft of the barn, but between the big jut of lava rock and the sagebrush and the twenty-two trees, you could find little niches where no one, nothing—not even the sky—could find you.

Sometimes up there under the cottonwood trees you could smell food cooking from the lean-to across the river: usually beef stew and sometimes pie or roast chicken. You could smell those things every once in a while, but not for very long, and you never heard a thing from where that woman Sugar Babe lived under the catalpa tree with the nigger—couldn't; it was too far away.

And there were times up there, too, under the cottonwood trees, when the wind was right, that you could hear old Harold P. Endicott's big American flag snapping in the wind, sounding like when the older guys would roll a wet towel and whip you a good one in physical-education class.

It wasn't far downstream from the stand of twenty-two cottonwood trees that Harold P. Endicott lived in his big house in his own cluster of trees. Even before the chinook blew in and everything started to happen, that house seemed haunted to me, and so did those five dogs of his that he lived alone with: five Dobermans—hellhounds—dogs even meaner than old Endicott himself, as it turned out. Those five hellhounds ate Harold P. Endicott alive in his very own home, the flag snapping away that night while it rained. After all that time the sky picked that night to open up and pour.

My father was too drunk that night to remember anything, and the nigger died after that, crows got to him, and dogs, not Harold P. Endicott's dogs—the sheriff shot those right off—but other dogs, strays, I guess, and that woman Sugar Babe had been dead for almost four months by then. And besides my father, Harold P. Endicott, and the nigger, there's only me to know. It was only the four of us there that night: my father, Harold P. Endicott, the nigger, and me. We were the only ones there besides the hellhounds.

After that first night of the chinook, nothing was ever the same. The chinook started it all in February, but it wasn't until that night in October that trouble showed itself outright, appeared to all of us like a ghost, like the Holy Ghost did at Pentecost, or angels, or the way Satan came to Jesus in the desert.

Harold P. Endicott had the deed to our farm in his Bank and Trust. With it being so dry that year, my father couldn't make but half the farm payment. My father had made the farm payment on the twenty-second of October for twelve years in a row without fail, but that year of the chinook, my father couldn't make but half the farm payment because of the drought, and Harold P. Endicott took our farm away, even though it only happened that one time after twelve whole years that my father could only come up with half.

They found Harold P. Endicott about a week after that, nine days to be exact, nine days after the twenty-second of October. On Halloween they found him, and they said Harold P. Endicott had probably been dead for about a week as far as they could tell from what was left of him. That's what I heard the sheriff say that evening in my room at the St. Anthony's Hospital: all that was left was a pile of bones.

They found the nigger the next night, on All Saints' Day, the day when all the saints disconnect themselves from heaven and search around for lost souls between here and there. That was the day—the night—that I snuck out of my room at the St. Anthony's Hospital because of what I had heard the sheriff say, and hitched a ride with Mona Lisa and Wolf and the rest of them in the Studebaker and went back to the farm in the hope of seeing the nigger again before we moved away to someplace like Rock Springs or Lava, or wherever my father decided to go; in the hope of seeing the nigger and asking him if he could tell me some more about illusion—how it was sometimes more than something you were always making up; and in the hope, too, of asking him if what we did that night in the rain with the hellhounds was the right thing to do.

One thing always leads to another, is another thing my mother always said. Then she would seal it. She'd say: forevermore. My mother was always saying: *one thing always leads to another,* then *forevermore.*

My mother said that and my father said this: *stay away from the river,* he said, *never swim in the river.* The river was a forbidden place and so was his saddle room; and he said to stay clear of Harold P. Endicott, and to stay clear of that woman Sugar Babe, and to stay clear of the nigger too.

Two forbidden places and three forbidden people.

I disobeyed my father with the river that summer that it got dry. I jumped in the river in June and kept on all summer because it was hot, because the river was so low, and because that summer I was older than I'd been. One thing always leads to another, and when I jumped in the river that first week in June, that jump led to other jumps, other swims, longer swims up the river, and down. It led to those other forbiddens, those three forbidden people: Harold P. Endicott, that woman Sugar Babe, and the nigger.

The day that I saw all three of them together was the day the trouble blown in by the chinook first started to show.

Before that day, there was a troubled feeling on things, like the world was drifting from that round-ball place where it was hanging in the sky; troubled air lying on you, troubled sky all around.

No rain after a winter of hardly any snow.

The horses paced around the fences of the corral, making a circle, pacing the manure into a hard round path on the ground inside the square. The pigs were always breaking down their pen and getting out, and in the coop the hens weren't laying as good. They sat on their eggs—wouldn't move off—and pecked at you when you tried to reach for them.

The tractor broke down.

My mother said she forgot how to sleep.

When you looked out the kitchen window in the afternoon, you could see puddles of water in the yard, but they weren't really puddles. They were heat waves—a mirage in the yard; illusion.

Mosquitoes at your ears at night.

And those hawks flying.

One morning I heard my mother let out a scream and I ran outside to her. There she stood on her patch of lawn. The lawn was covered with dandelions. Every day my mother went out there, and after she watered the Virginia creepers and the Seven Sisters rose on the trellis, she dug dandelion roots up out of that patch of lawn of hers with the paring knife, and the day before, there had not been one single dandelion there in the grass. Then that morning she screamed, there they were: on her patch of lawn like a plague.

The day that I saw those three forbidden people together—Harold P. Endicott, that woman Sugar Babe, and the nigger—was the first time that I had ever actually seen the nigger, but it wasn't the first time that

I had seen Sugar Babe. It wasn't my first time for seeing Harold P. Endicott either.

Twice before, on my swing, I had seen that woman Sugar Babe leave the lean-to on the other side of the river under the catalpa tree, and both times she was in a yellow dress, carrying a big yellow hat with a wide brim. I could see that her black hair was long and thick. It shined. I could see that she was wearing high heels, yellow high heels. What I could actually see was that her shoes were yellow, I couldn't see that her shoes were high heels, but I could tell that they were by the way she walked. She walked the way my mother walked when my mother wore her high heels with the holes in the toes on Sunday.

That woman walked up the wooden planks to her old '49 Ford and got in the old Ford and drove off to the Working Man's Club with the blue half-moon in the window on West Center Street in Wind River, where she was a waitress. Sugar Babe in her yellow dress, in her yellow wide-brimmed hat, in her yellow high heels walking like that in a Negro bar, waitressing, serving martinis to Montgomery Clift, who sat at the bar in a suit with thin lapels, hunched over one of those special kind of glasses, smoking.

The only time I saw old Harold P. Endicott before that day that I saw all three of them together was in the Grand Entry of the Wind River Frontier Rodeo with the rest of the Matisse County Mounted Posse. I was in the grandstand with my mother when Harold P. Endicott rode in on an Appaloosa mare leading the other men on their horses through the figure eight. The shiny dark green material of his posse shirt had two big dark wet spots under the arms and a long dark wet spot down the middle of the back. In front, the buttons strained to cinch him all in. The silver whistle that called his hellhounds hung on a chain around his neck. *Lard ass* my mother said, and I laughed when she said it because I had only heard her say *damn* once when she said *damned old souse,* and *son of a bitch* twice when the pigs got out and jumped in the river. I had never heard her say *ass* before, and I had never laughed before when I heard her swear—at least not in front of her. And I had never heard her say any kind of swear word before without putting the Sign of the Cross with it pretty soon after. That day when she said *lard ass* at the Wind River Frontier Rodeo—meaning Harold P. Endicott—was the first time I ever saw her not cross herself. When I laughed out loud she looked at me sideways for a minute, but then she ended up laughing too.

You could tell by the way Harold P. Endicott wore his Stetson hat that he had no hair because his hat came right down to his eyes like a Stetson hat on a trailer hitch, and he squinted his eyes like he was always looking at the toolshed. The squint screwed up his whole round pink face. After my mother said it, I'd look at him and couldn't think anything but *lard ass.*

And when the Grand Entry was over, the posse in their shiny green shirts faced the grandstand in formation, all of them lined up sitting tall in their saddles. In front of them there were two more posse men on horseback presenting the Idaho state flag and the Matisse County posse flag, and in front of those two, centered between them, was old Harold P. Endicott carrying the American flag. Old Glory snapped at the end of his pole. Harold P. Endicott took the Stetson off his head and that must have been the signal. Once Endicott showed his bald, sweaty head, the two men behind him took their hats off, and then the straight line of posse members to the rear took theirs off and then all the men and all the cowgirls in the grandstand with hats, took them off. Everybody put their hats on their chests when Harold P. Endicott put his hat on his, and then the organist in the announcer's stand started playing "The Star-Spangled Banner," and we all sang—sang about how America was there in the sky in the twilight, sang about rockets and the red glare and proof through the night. We sang through the waves of dust, things smelling like horse turds, cow manure, fried onions and hot dogs; people sang with their hats on their hearts, sang their heads off with Endicott's Old Glory snapping, the animals nervous, the Shoshone-Bannock hoop dancers nervous, drinking Thunderbird behind the back pens, under the grandstand, and in their beat-up cars in the parking lot. The steers and bulls and calves and clowns' trick dogs restless and penned up and hog-tied and caged—every person and creature restless for what always comes after that song: the snap of the gate, the bursting in air, whips, spurs in the flesh, ropes that burned the hide, that choked.

Brave we sang, and free.

The saddle room, my father's saddle room, was in the barn. Its door was always locked, but just from peeking under that door you could see how the cement was swept clean. There was no straw, no dust, not ever. The door was made of two-by-eights—six of them—and creaked like the *Inner Sanctum* door on the radio when my father pulled it open by its leather strap. My father kept the key to his saddle-room door in the little pocket on the right side of his Levi's. The extra key he hid under a board in the feed manger next to the red radio he used to listen to when he milked the cows.

I never went into that saddle room. I disobeyed my father about the river that dry summer that I was older, and with one thing leading to another like it does, I ran into those other forbiddens, those three forbidden people, but I never did disobey my father when it came to the saddle room. Not once did I set foot into that place—his secret place—not ever, that is, until that night that I got myself out of that room in the St. Anthony's Hospital and hitched a ride back to the farm with Wolf and Mona Lisa and the others in the Studebaker; not until that night that I found the nigger hanging there. And after I realized what it was, who it was that was hanging, and after I could think and walk again, I walked straight to the red radio and got that key out from under the board in the feed manger, and unlocked the saddle-room door. I walked right in there and turned on the light and went straight to the drawer where I knew his secret was. The drawer was locked so I took the twelve-gauge and cocked it and blew a hole in the drawer and then reached right in there and took my father's secret out; opened the manila envelope, took it out, took them all out and had a good look.

After all that time standing outside that locked door, finally I was holding the secret in my hands; I was inside the secret room, opened by the secret key hidden in a secret place.

It wasn't a place I'd ever expected to be.

But I knew what to expect once I was in there. Oh, I knew about his guns in there; his .22, his .25-20, his twelve-gauge. I knew about his saddles and his bridles, and his saddle blankets and his curry combs. I knew that he made outlines on the wall of things hanging on the wall so that when you took a curry comb down or the twelve-gauge down, their outlines in red were left on the wall like red haloes. For some strange, secret reason, he did that—made red haloes of his things on the wall. I knew about this stuff because once he slipped up and left the door open. I went over to the door and stood there at the threshold looking in for half a minute or so before I locked it up again. In those thirty-some seconds I felt like I felt in the St. Joseph's Church at Our Mother of Perpetual Help Devotions when Monsignor Canby put the Body of Christ in the monstrance and turned to the congregation with God in his hands and I was kneeling below him on the stairs ringing the Gloria bells. That's how I felt looking in there, into my father's place, like I was a footstep away from trespassing on some holy place, or maybe like I was lying flat on the cookie sheet with a ripple in it, staring at the sky; but even more than that, because the feeling I had way down deep in me was as bright as the toolshed without a shadow: I was looking into the mystery of my father's awful, secret ways.

After all those years that I had studied my father as faithfully as catechism: his Stetson hat tilted back, strands of black hair wet against his forehead; him in the barn, me hidden behind the post among the cobwebs, the milk strainers, and the bag balm, NBC on the red radio tuned to Dinah Washington or Tennessee Ernie Ford, the suction cups sucking the teats of black-and-white cows, my father's fingers working their nipples, the gold of his wedding band pressed against cowhide; him in the toolshed banging on hot red iron, bright sparks flying from the welder, I could not look.

I knew his smell, too, at close quarters with my father in the house, in the bathroom after he got done. It was only how he always smelled, but stronger, like his boots and his socks that he left on the back porch and by the stove in winter. Sometimes his smell was mixed with Old Spice, usually on Saturday nights and on Sunday mornings driving to nine-o'clock Mass.

But after standing so long before that locked door, after locking it back up that one time he left it open, there I was that night after I found the nigger: holding my father's secret in my hands.

❧ ❧

That day that I saw all three of them together was one of those days that came about from one thing leading to another: jumping in the river, swimming upstream, sitting in the water in the narrow spot by the jut of lava rock just down from the dog-leg where the water was fast. That day I moved farther upstream than I'd been—to the wide place in the river where the dead limb of the catalpa tree got stuck on a gravel bar. I was sitting on that dead catalpa branch thinking about things, not any one thing in particular, just letting one thought lead to another, when I heard a woman scream. I didn't realize until I heard the scream how close I was to the catalpa tree and the lean-to. I ducked down and looked over that way—the way of the scream—and I saw that woman Sugar Babe come flying out the back door of the lean-to and land on the ground, her long black shiny hair down around her waist, with only her brassiere on and her panties on. That brassiere and panties were white against her brown skin. She came flying out the back door of the lean-to, her hair flying, because he had hit her. Harold P. Endicott had hit that woman Sugar Babe. I knew for sure it was Harold P. Endicott because then he came out the door right after her. She managed to get up and then Endicott hit her again; she was screaming as she fell down in the dirt. Harold P. Endicott started pointing his finger at her like the Holy Cross nuns do to you at the St. Joseph's School and he was yelling at her and using those swear words men use. Then he kicked her in the stomach and went to kick her again, when suddenly the nigger jumped on him from behind. The men struggled like that for a long time, the both of them yelling terrible and cussing at each other, the nigger's right arm around Endicott's neck and his left hand smacking at Endicott's face and chest, Endicott bent over, his Stetson hat knocked off, his pink head pointing at me fat and round. All the while that woman Sugar Babe was screaming and cussing like usually only men do, saying all those words, and then I saw Endicott put the whistle that was hanging around his neck into his mouth. There was a high-pitched sound, the sound I think the planets must make as they whirl in their orbits around the sun in infinity, an awful, other-worldly sound, and then those hell-hounds came around the corner of the house and jumped on that woman Sugar Babe and the nigger.

I dived and swam downriver, staying underwater as far as I could, holding my breath, my heart beating everywhere, and in my chest a pain—from not breathing and their screams.

Their screams were the worst sounds that I had ever heard: that woman Sugar Babe and the nigger screaming, scared and mad and crying out like lost souls.

Running through the cottonwoods, I could hear their screams still. I could hear the dogs on top of them, teeth biting into their flesh. As I swam, as I ran, I was thinking those dogs were after me. I could feel their teeth on my calves and ankles. I ran and ran and I could hear them the whole time: the hellhounds, the screams of that woman, the screams of the nigger and what he was calling out to her, to that woman Sugar Babe.

Mother, he was calling out to her.

Mother is what the nigger was screaming out to Sugar Babe, to that woman. *Mother, Mother.*

That night, lying in bed, I couldn't stop thinking about the hellhounds, and about Harold P. Endicott, and about that woman Sugar Babe and the nigger; couldn't stop hearing the nigger calling out to her, calling out *Mother* like that.

I tried praying the rosary again but I was too nervous to keep track of the beads.

But more than anything, what I was thinking was that I had run away.

Nobody was allowed to read the newspaper before my father read the newspaper, and that night, two days after I saw the three of them together—Harold P. Endicott, that woman Sugar Babe, and the nigger—when I came in for supper that night, my mother had put the newspaper on the coffee table next to my father's chair like usual. I looked over and this was the headline: "BODY OF WOMAN FOUND IN PORTNEUF RIVER."

I picked up the newspaper without thinking and then put it back down because nobody was allowed to read the newspaper before my father read the newspaper. My father always read the newspaper after supper with his coffee, usually in the front room or, when it was hot, on the front porch.

"What's wrong?" my mother said when she saw me. She had been asking me that for two days.

"Nothing," I told her as I had all along.

"Something's bothering you," my mother said. "Has been for two days now."

"Nothing's bothering me." But I was acting bothered and lied again.

My mother just looked at me and put the tuna casserole on the supper table—it was Friday again—but that Friday my father wouldn't eat the tuna casserole because my mother had tried something new and put potato chips in it, so my mother scrambled him up some eggs and spuds, which he did eat.

All through supper she watched me with that look on her face—that same look she had that first night of the chinook when she swept past the bathroom door.

There's not much you can do when my mother turns that eye on you but let yourself be watched, so I concentrated on my tuna casserole and had part of a second helping. I didn't like tuna casserole much either, and my mother knew it, so I took part of a second helping to let her know that I knew she was watching me and also to let her know that the potato chips helped out some.

I watched as my father left the supper table when he got done eating his spuds and eggs. I saw in my head how he walked down the hallway of the butterflies and the dice, and into the front room, where he picked up the newspaper that my mother had folded for him and placed on the coffee table, and, because the evening was so hot, how my father went out onto the front porch. There was no screen on the front door, and no screen-door spring to make any kind of sound. My mother poured my father's coffee for him, stirred the two sugars in, cut him a piece of rhubarb pie, and took them out to him on the front porch. When my mother came back into the kitchen, she unplugged the percolator and poured herself a cup of coffee and set the cup on the table. Then she went back to the stove and cut me a piece of rhubarb pie and asked me again what was wrong. I didn't say anything until after I finished my pie; then I just shrugged my shoulders and still didn't say anything because how do you start telling your mother something that begins with one thing that led to another? Just where do you start with something like that?

The only way that you can begin is at the beginning. And so I finally began: "I have been swimming in the Portneuf pretty near all summer now," I said, and looked at her. My mother looked back at me.

And then my father walked in the door with the newspaper in his hand and said this, all at once, "That woman, that Injun woman cross the river, the one they call Sugar Babe, who lives with that nigger over there, well, they found her naked and floating in the river, dead. Been there a couple of days, it says here. Says there wasn't much left of her, that some dogs or coyotes probably got to her in the river. And it says the nigger she lives with over there in that lean-to is missing. They got a posse out right now looking for that nigger. Says here they think the nigger probably killed her." And then he said what he always said. "Always trouble with those kind of people. They just got a nose for it."

My father then looked at my mother and my mother looked at my father and then my mother looked back at me, her eye way off somewhere else, and then she crossed herself. I looked at my father and then we all looked at each other.

"Your son's been swimming in the Portneuf," my mother said to my father. "And one thing always leads to another." Then she said, "Forevermore," and she crossed herself again.

"Harold P. Endicott killed her, killed that woman Sugar Babe," I said.

"What were you doing in that river?" my father said. He dropped the paper on the floor.

"Endicott hit her and she fell down and then the nigger jumped on top of Endicott and then Endicott whistled for his dogs, and his dogs attacked that woman and the nigger," I said.

"Didn't I tell you to stay out of that river?" my father said.

"The nigger didn't kill her, Endicott killed her, his hellhounds killed her."

"What were you doing in the Portneuf?" my father said. "I told you not to go in the river."

"The nigger didn't kill her, I know it. It was Endicott who did it. She was his mother."

"Who was his mother?" my mother said.

"That woman, Sugar Babe," I said.

"Whose mother?" my mother said.

"The nigger's! He wouldn't kill his mother." My mother's left eye started to drift.

"How do you know she was his mother?" my father asked.

"That's what the nigger called her when the dogs was on them." I said.

"Forevermore!" my mother said, and crossed herself.

"None of this would have happened if you'd stayed out of the river," my father said.

"Nigger's probably dead too," I said, and then there was a silence and my father looked at the floor, at the headlines on the newspaper lying there. My mother was looking too. Those words seemed like they were bigger than even my father in the room right then; bigger than all of us: WOMAN DEAD. It was quiet for a while longer and then my father told my mother to leave us alone.

"What you going to do?" my mother asked my father. My father looked at her strange and he leaned back a little, like I'd seen him lean back when his own mother, Grandma Ruth, talked to him, and he got a hurt look on his face that my mother could ask such a question. My mother was standing up and we were both sitting down, my father and I, looking at my mother.

"This boy's too old to give a licking to, but I'm going to," my father said.

"The boy didn't do nothing," my mother said.

"He jumped in the river!" my father said, and stood up fast, kicking the chair back, "and I told him to stay clear of that river and those people. Now, just look at this mess!" my father said, moving his face right up against hers.

They stood there like that, the two of them, my mother and my father, squared off, my father's hands becoming fists.

"You're going to lose that boy," my mother said. "You can't beat that boy for this."

"Mary," my father said. I had never heard my father call my mother that. "Leave us alone now. This is not a woman's concern."

The way my father said "Mary" like that and "woman" like that, did it. My mother turned and walked over to where she kept the silverware and got the paring knife out of the drawer. Then she walked outside through the kitchen door, and the way she looked walking out, the way the kitchen door opened, reminded me again of the night of the chinook.

My father took his belt off and told me to drop my pants; told me to bend over and hold on to the edge of the supper table and drop my pants, just like he had told me to do other times.

I wanted to say something big then. I wanted to use those words he used when my mother wasn't around—use them to say something big.

But I held my breath, like I had all those other times in the past, and dropped my pants and my shorts, my back to him, and leaned over and grabbed on to the edge of the supper table.

Other times, my father would have hit me three or four times right off and I would have had my pants back up in nothing flat and neither of us would have said anything for a bit. Then he'd say something like *don't ever do that again,* or *shape up or ship out,* but that was when I was younger.

This time, as I stood there like that, waiting, nothing happened. I turned to see what was up, and saw in my father's face something I had never seen there before. I don't know what it was, but his face was red and he was blinking, and when he saw me turn, he hit me twice—harder than other times, harder than ever before—and I felt awful enough to puke.

"I'm ashamed of you," my father said. "Pull your pants up!" he said.

I didn't want to move because it hurt, but I did what he told me to do. I turned around, faced him, and pulled up my shorts, and then my pants. His face got redder and he was still blinking and he did something else then too. Something new. His upper lip quivered a little, though you could tell he was trying to act like his lip wasn't doing that.

It was then that I realized my awful feeling was a feeling for him, not for me, and that *I'm ashamed of you,* is what I should have been saying then to him. So I looked him straight in the eye, and I did say it: *I'm ashamed of you,* not out loud, but in my head, and even though I didn't say it right out, I got my point across.

"Let me educate you about this mother stuff," my father said. "Even though you should know things like this already by now," he said. "Those people, them niggers, got a way of talking. They use that word 'mother' different from how we use it. When they say 'mother' what they're really saying is 'mother*fucker.*' That's just their way."

My father's face wasn't red anymore. He wasn't blinking and his lip was back to normal. "Now, I don't have to tell you what 'motherfucker' means, do I?" my father said.

We were still eye to eye, my father and me. "No," I said, "you don't have to tell me. I know what it means."

My father told me to go to my room and not to come back out until he told me to. I walked out of the kitchen into the hall of butterflies and dice and went upstairs. I closed the door to my room hard, but I didn't slam it. A temper wasn't allowed in the house, or anywhere near my parents. I went straight for my window and opened it up all the way. I was going to slide down the eave to the trellis with the Seven Sisters rose hanging on it, and climb down and get right out of there, get away from him, get away from my father. I was thinking about going to California or Broadway—any place faraway—but deep down I knew I'd probably settle for my swing up in the cottonwoods.

Just then the sheriff drove his Jeep into the yard, and not long after the sheriff drove in, the Matisse County Mounted Posse rode in on their horses—no shiny shirts this time, no American flag, and no Harold P. Endicott. The sheriff shut off his Jeep and the men on horses gathered around.

My mother got up quick-like from the lawn where she had been digging dandelions up by their roots, and walked into the house. I heard the screen door slam, then the murmur of my mother and father talking downstairs. The screen door slammed again, and from my window I saw my father walking toward those men.

"'Evening, Joe!" the sheriff said loud and friendly so everyone could hear. "How's everything?"

"Can't complain, Bill," my father said. "That is, if the wind don't blow us away!"

"Yup, she's as dry as a bone," the sheriff said.

"Don't look good," my father said.

A couple of men in the posse said hello to my father and my father said hello back. *Hello, Clyde. Hello, Sam. Hello, Jeff. Hello, Jay. Hello, Eric. Hello, J.D.*

"What you guys up to? Looking for trouble?" my father said.

"Yeah, trouble," the sheriff said. "We're looking for the nigger. You seen this evening's paper?"

"Yeah, I saw it," my father said. "Was just reading about it. Those people got a nose for trouble."

"Hell, Joe, you know that ain't the part of them that gets them into trouble!" the sheriff said, and all the men laughed and my father laughed too.

"You seen him around here?" the sheriff asked.

"Nope," my father said.

"How about the rest of your family, your wife, Mary, she seen him?" the sheriff asked.

"Nope," my father said.

"How about that strapping son of yours, he seen him?" the sheriff asked.

"Nope," my father said. "He ain't seen him neither."

August that year was like the toolshed at noon. There was no wind, just the sun hot overhead, too bright, drying out everything, burning up shadows. Even at night, it was never really dark; things still had that sun in them and they glowed like stars, like those kinds of rosaries and statues of Jesus, Mary, and Joseph that glow in the dark. Once in a while there was thunder and lightning, but never rain. The dogs would howl and those hawks just kept flying, even in the dark.

I was like that too, like those hot nights in August: burning up, thunder and lightning from down there shooting up to my brain, me in my bed sweating away and staining things yellow. My mother just couldn't wash that yellow out, and I knew that she tried. She'd soak my shorts in the kitchen sink in Clorox and bluing for the whole day.

I wanted to stop—stop yellowing things up—because it was a mess and a sin and I had to count the times and tell Monsignor Canby about every occasion, tick off those sins like the red triangle flags snapping, marking the miles, in the wind. Mortal, every one of them, mortal, every time. But I just couldn't stop the yellowing or the counting neither, couldn't stop counting the red flags. I couldn't let up, just like the sun couldn't that August.

That year the Blackfoot State Fair was in August, the last week. We always went to the Blackfoot State Fair:

my mother, my father, and me. Usually we would get up early and drive to Blackfoot and go to the fair and spend the whole day there and then see the fireworks in the grandstand that night and stay overnight at my Grandma Hannah's—my mother's mother—then go back home the next morning.

I always used to look forward to the Blackfoot State Fair, used to count the days to go on the calendar, crossing them off. But that year, that year of the chinook, that dry, hot, river-jumping, staining-things-yellow year of those three forbidden people, the year my father lied to the sheriff, was different. I didn't even want to go to the Blackfoot State Fair that year. I wanted them—my mother and my father—to go to the Blackfoot State Fair without me. But my father wouldn't hear of it. I went and did those things like I did every year that I used to like to do and hated now: I put on my black polished Sunday shoes and red socks and my new stiff Levi's—washed only once—and the new shirt my mother bought me at J. C. Penney's: short-sleeved and blue that looked like it was two shirts—a blue plaid shirt under a solid blue vest—but it wasn't. It was all one shirt, and I rolled up the sleeves. I put my toothbrush in with the rest of the bathroom stuff that my mother put in a plastic bag, and a change of underwear, and I got in the back seat of the Oldsmobile. My father drove—he always drove—and we bought Cokes and RC Colas at the Wyz-Way market like we always did and I got a Snickers, and my mother wanted me to sing those same old songs with her:

"Faith, Hope, and Charity" and "Going to the Chapel and We're Going to Get Married." I sang along, all right, but I didn't like it. I wanted to listen to the radio, to the rock-and-roll station.

For the first time that year, as I sang away in the back seat, I wondered why the old man, why my father, never sang with us. Other years, when my mother and I sang those old dumb songs, we were singing for him. We were entertaining him. Seems like everything my mother and I did was for him, and that year, that August, things were different. I was older and figured out what was going on and didn't like it.

Why couldn't he come up with a song once? Now, *that* would be entertaining.

When we got to Blackfoot, there was a lot of traffic and it took a long time to get to the main gate. Then once we got to the main gate, we had to park the Oldsmobile way out there in the sun. It took us a long time to get to the barns, and when we did, we were all covered with dust, and there wasn't any decent place for my mother to freshen up.

But none of those things were really that much bother—at least they didn't bother me. What did bother me at the Blackfoot State Fair was the same thing that bothered me every year. My mother and my father always seemed to pick the Blackfoot State Fair to be mad at each other—be mad and stay mad. Until that year, my mother and father only got mad at each other at the Blackfoot State Fair.

When they were mad at each other, my mother and

my father didn't act or talk any way different from the usual, although my father's voice got higher and my mother's got lower and my mother smoked my father's Viceroys in front of him. They still talked to each other, but they didn't say much. My mother said her usual things—*you want another ice cube, Dad,* stuff like that—and my father gave his usual answers: *Yeah, Mom, I'll have one,* or *nope,* and just drive and smoke Viceroys.

What got different when my mother and my father were mad at each other was the world; everything and everybody else was a little off—a touch cantankerous, and full of bother. My mother called it *the devil's work,* and crossed herself when she said *devil,* but crossing herself didn't stop the mischief. Everybody drove like they were from Utah, the Cokes weren't cold enough, and somebody always got to the perfect parking space before us, or just as we pulled up, the traffic cop put his hand out so we had to stop and let everybody else and their dog go ahead.

My mother's eye got cockeyed when she was mad at my father at the Blackfoot State Fair, but not like that way it had the night of the chinook. Both eyes went slightly off, slightly askew—her right eye, not just the left eye.

My mother kept saying *forevermore,* and my father made that clucking sound with his tongue, said those words under his breath, and turned his knuckles white gripping the steering wheel.

Other years, when we went to the Blackfoot State

Fair, I used to try to do things to keep them from being mad at each other, tried to keep the conversation going, making comments about things I noticed: how straight the barbed wire next to the road was, what a neat car just passed us, how nice my mother's singing voice was, though it wasn't all that great.

But that year I didn't bother with any of that kind of stuff. I just let it go the way it always got anyway.

My mother said it was a crying shame the way the crops looked on display on the counters in the vegetable barns that year. *A crying shame,* she said, *forevermore.* The sugar beets and the potatoes were half the size of the year before, and the garden vegetables—the carrots and string beans and acorn squash—were a disgrace. *The sheaves of wheat should be as tall as you are,* my father said, meaning as tall as me. But that year they were knee-high, maybe even shorter.

In the cow barns, things were a little better. The cattle and the pigs and the sheep all seemed fat and sassy like other years, and their troughs were full of water, but all everybody could talk about was the drought and how hard it was to get feed, and for a decent price. Everywhere it was the same sorry story.

When we got through with looking at the crops and the animals, usually we would go to the canned-goods part, then the arts-and-crafts section, where there was quilting and embroidery and fruit drying out; then we would go to where the machinery was and wait while my father talked combines and beet toppers and grain drills with the John Deere man. That's usually how it went. We usually did the machinery right after the crops and animals and canned goods and arts and crafts, and that year was no different. My father's eyes lit up soon as he saw those shiny new green John Deere machines. He headed straight for them, and everything seemed the way it had always been at the Blackfoot State Fair. But then my mother gave me two dollars and told me not to tell my father she'd given me the money. Then she told me to take off out of there and have a good time before it was too late to have any more good times. I looked at those two dollar bills in my hand and asked her what time I should be back by. *It's a small world,* my mother said, and *you're not getting away from me that easy. There's plenty of time to worry about time,* she said. I hugged my mother, fast, and was all of a sudden very sad for her, things starting to seem suddenly different than usual at the Blackfoot State Fair. I hugged her fast, right there by the new three-bottom John Deere plow, and took off.

I got my hand stamped when I left the fairgrounds so I could get back in, and I walked down Main Street Blackfoot, past the courthouse and past Klegg's Used Furniture Store where my mother and my father had bought my bed. I walked right into the Oasis Bar and bought a bottle of Schlitz and a pack of Lucky Strikes. I didn't want to buy Viceroys; they had filters. The bartender was an old woman, half-blind, and I think she was drunk. She gave me back too much change, but rather than say anything, I just left the difference—fifteen cents—on the counter there.

I wanted to ask the guys in there if any of them had seen the nigger. Ever since that day I saw those three people together, the day I saw Harold P. Endicott sic those hellhounds on that woman Sugar Babe and the nigger, ever since then I don't think I ever stopped thinking about the nigger and where he might be.

There were others of them in the Oasis Bar—other Negro men—and some Sho-Ban Indians too, and I wanted to ask them about the nigger, but what could I say? How could I begin? *Hello, where's the nigger? Did you know that woman Sugar Babe?* So I just got a sack for the beer and rolled the cigarettes in my sleeve like the big guys did at the high school and I walked to the railroad park, chugging the beer and smoking a Lucky Strike.

After I finished them both—the beer and the cigarette—I kind of got sick and dizzy. I puked, but after I puked I felt better. I felt better than I'd ever felt, and I went back that way, feeling better than I had ever felt. I went back to the Blackfoot State Fair, but not to the cows and pigs and pickled beets and quilting demonstrations. I went back to where the rides were, and the sideshows, to the places where you could throw a ball and win things. I took the cigarettes out of my sleeve, just in case I ran into my mother or father. I put the pack down there, in my underwear, in my yellow underwear. For some reason, saying yellow underwear to myself like that really made me laugh that day.

I rode theTilt-O-Whirl and the Ferris Wheel and the Rocket Plane, the Mix Master, and the Snake. I won a Kewpie doll for my mother and a pair of dice for my father and bought pink cotton candy and a Pronto Pup with mustard.

One of those women who sell you tickets in the booth asked me how come I was having so much fun. Her skin was dark, like Sugar Babe's, and she wore a scarf that hid her hair but not her big gold earrings. For a minute I thought she was Sugar Babe. I wanted to light up a Lucky Strike and say something neat, something neat like maybe Marlon Brando or Montgomery Clift would say, but my Lucky Strikes were in my pants and I never was very good at talking, so I just said something dumb like *'cause it's the state fair,* something really dumb like that. Then I took off out of there.

And then there was the man, one of those guys who takes your ticket and then straps you in—into the Rocket Plane, I think—and when he strapped me in, he touched me down there on my Lucky Strikes and asked me how my hammer was hanging. He had tattoos on his arms. I didn't answer. I spent my time on the Rocket Plane knowing what the guy with the tattoos meant when he said what he said about hammers. I was pretty sure I knew, all right. When the Rocket Plane came back down, he unstrapped me and went for my Lucky Strikes again. I almost fell over the platform trying to get out of there.

That's when I saw the magician, the one who called himself Mr. Energy. Mr. Energy pulled white doves out of a black hat, and changed them into crows just by putting them in a box and tapping the box with his magic wand. He cut a woman in half with an electric saw—I could barely watch—and then put her back together again. He also took a rope and hung himself by the neck. His assistant, a dwarf, walked under him to show the audience that there was no trick, that Mr. Energy had really hung himself and was dead, but the curtain fell and in nothing flat went up again, and Mr. Energy was hanging there from his feet. In no time, he reached up and untied himself and took a bow while everyone clapped. Then he and the dwarf took a bow together and the curtain went down for good.

Right after the clapping was over and the audience was getting up to leave, Mr. Energy came out from behind the curtain and walked up to the edge of the stage. He started talking to us as if he was talking to a bunch of his friends. Mr. Energy looked each person straight in the eye as he spoke. He looked me straight in the eye especially, and for a long time. My ears went haywire and I got that feeling like when I saw a rattlesnake one day when I was up in the cottonwoods swinging in the swing—the feeling that something awful could get to you wherever you were.

Mr. Energy's eyes got real wide so you could see white all around the colored part. "Everything is an illusion!" he said. "Not just up here on the stage, not just in the circus." Mr. Energy said, "*Everything* is an illusion."

And then Mr. Energy asked me, or told me, rather, singled me out of the whole audience like that, and told me to repeat what he had just said.

"Everything is an illusion." I said what he told me to say.

And then Mr. Energy said, "Do you think that statement is a true statement, young man?"

I said, "I guess so."

And Mr. Energy said, "Well, it is!" Then Mr. Energy said, "What is your name, young man?"

"Jacob Joseph Weber," I said.

"Well, Mr. Jacob Joseph Weber," Mr. Energy said, "tell me, do you understand what illusion is?"

I was pretty nervous. I'd never had a famous person talk to me like that, especially in front of all those people. I didn't know what to say, so I just said, "Yes."

Everybody in the audience kind of chuckled and then Mr. Energy said, "Well, tell me what it is, then, Mr. Jacob Joseph Weber. Tell me what illusion is!"

"It is everything." I said. "Illusion is all there is."

But the best thing that happened that day, better even than Mr. Energy talking to me instead of to any of those other people he could have talked to, better than the Schlitz, the Lucky Strikes, better than buying the Schlitz and the Lucky Strikes, better than the woman selling tickets and the tattooed guy at the Rocket Plane, maybe the best thing ever was this: I saw the nigger.

I was in the Hall of Mirrors when I got lost. Actually, I didn't get lost in the Hall of Mirrors at all—you'd have to be pretty dumb to get lost in the Hall of Mirrors. There was nothing to it: just two hallways with different kinds of mirrors along the walls and loud music blaring. Where I got lost was when I went through the door that said *No Exit*. The door locked behind me and it was pitch black. I was in there for a good long time trying to find my way out, stumbling around in a room that was long and narrow and so dark I couldn't see my hand when I put it right in front of my eyes. I was scared by the time I found a doorknob behind a curtain. I turned that knob and pushed hard. The door flung open and I almost lost my balance. There I stood in the sunlight. Sunlight was pouring through that door. After my eyes got used to the bright, I looked down and there was the nigger, sitting back behind the trailer that was the Hall of Mirrors, sitting there on a bale of straw, smoking.

I was never so happy as then.

The nigger looked up at me, startled. I could tell he knew right off who I was. I wondered how he did. He smiled at first, then got a scared look on his face. I jumped down fast out that back door of the Hall of Mirrors and slammed the door behind me. I thought for sure the nigger was going to run, so I yelled *don't run away* and waved my arms, dropping the Kewpie doll in the dust. The nigger was about ready to jump the barbed-wire fence, but he stopped and turned when I yelled. I unbuttoned my Levi's. The buttons were hard because the Levi's were new, but I finally pulled the Lucky Strikes out of my shorts, put one of them in my mouth, lit it, and inhaled, just like I had seen the nigger inhaling. Then I tried to button up my Levi's again.

The nigger started laughing—laughing in a way I had never seen anybody laugh before—shaking all over, like all he was was laughter. With him laughing like that, he got me going too. Then the nigger said he had to pee, he was laughing so hard, only he said *piss,* not *pee*. He turned around and pissed, leaning up against the tree there, still laughing and pissing and trying not to get any on himself. I started coughing. I wasn't used to Lucky Strikes. Pretty soon I had to piss too, like the nigger. So there we were: together, the both of us, pissing and laughing, only I was coughing too, because of the Lucky Strike. Pissing there on dirt as fine as Johnson & Johnson baby powder, I pissed a small round circle, then tried to keep my aim straight in there in the center. And I did it—kept my aim straight—until I was about done, that is. Then I started dribbling.

When me and the nigger finally settled back down and weren't laughing anymore, it was quiet back there between us behind the Hall of Mirrors—strangely quiet because there seemed so much to say. As usual, I just didn't know where to begin. So, while I thought about the things I wanted to say and the best way to say them, all around us there were the sounds of the circus part of the Blackfoot State Fair: the generator for the Hall of Mirrors, the screams of girls riding the Tilt-O-Whirl, shouts from people riding the Snake and the Mix Master. Then there was that haywire sound in my ears again, like I got when Mr. Energy first started talking to me; the same sound I heard when I was in the swing up in the cottonwoods and saw the rattlesnake.

There were two small trees back there behind the Hall of Mirrors—elm trees with sparrows in their branches. Those trees gave some shade to the bales of straw. The nigger walked over and sat back down on one of the bales under the trees. I went over there too—I wasn't sure I should do it, but I went ahead and sat down right next to the nigger.

There were scars on his arms and hands that the hellhounds made.

Just as I sat down, the nigger got up. The nigger got up, took three steps away, then stopped dead. He didn't turn to face me, and I knew he was going to bolt any minute. I tried to think of something to make him stay. There was so much I wanted to ask him: how he had got away from the hellhounds, about *mother* and *motherfucker,* but all I could do was sit there and look at his black skin, the scars across it, and where there weren't any scars, where his skin was smooth and hairless as a black river stone.

The nigger turned his black rattlesnake eyes on me. His lips were pink on the inside, like bubble gum, and the palms of his hands pink too, but not the pink Endicott's skin was. The lines of the nigger's palm were as black as the rest of him.

I didn't know what else to do to make him stay, so for some reason, I don't know why, I just blurted out my secret name. "Haji Baba," I said. "My name is Haji Baba."

Once I had said it, said my secret name out loud, I felt red all over. To hear my name out loud like that—my name that only the hawks and the pigeons and the cottonwoods knew—made me sorry to have said it. It sounded like a name a child would call himself, like the name of a geek in a sideshow, not the name of a real man. I thought the nigger would laugh. I hated that he was going to laugh like the big guys did in physical-education class, in the locker rooms after class, like my father laughed, the way I guess the men in the posse laugh, the way the sheriff and Endicott laugh for sure. I hated that I had ever given myself that name, a silly kid's name, a girl's name. I hated even more that I had just blurted it out like that, not making any sense in front of the nigger. *Haji Baba, Haji Baba* went around in my head like *liar, liar, pants on fire.* I wished to God that I would finally grow up and stop making up silly names; wished to God that I would learn to think straight and not blurt dumb things out like I just did with *Haji Baba*.

Snakes can hypnotize you with their eyes and that's what I thought the nigger was doing to me, looking at me that way. The haywire sound was getting louder and louder, and then, suddenly, the nigger spoke: "And my name is Geronimo," he said without laughing, without moving his eyes. Then he smiled, warm and friendly. The world got flat as a cookie sheet and the sky became a bright dome. The light filtering through the tree leaves made the nigger look like those pictures of Jesus with a halo around his head.

And then he left. He disappeared around the Hall of Mirrors trailer. I ran after him and touched him on the shoulder, but he didn't want me to touch him or be around him anymore.

"She was your *mother,* wasn't she?" I said.

The nigger looked at me like he hated me then. He doubled up his fists and stepped toward me and I thought for sure he was going to hit me. But he stopped.

I started to tell him that I knew, that I had seen what the hellhounds had done to his mother, that I had tried to help but couldn't because I was too scared, and after, because no one would listen to Haji Baba. I wanted to ask him to take me with him so he could tell me about things, about feelings coming up strong from down there like that, because he knew about those kinds of things. I could tell. And he knew about things like the chinook and probably about one thing leading to another and illusion and important things like how far it is from the tip of a hummingbird's wing to its heart.

I didn't know, and I didn't ask him. Instead I gave him the rest of my money—twenty-eight cents—and the Lucky Strikes. The nigger's hands weren't fists anymore and he didn't look like he hated me. He took the twenty-eight cents and the Lucky Strikes, said *thank you,* and was gone.

When I found my mother it was at the Catholic Women's Booth. I gave her the Kewpie doll and she liked it, but my father didn't. "Waste of good money," he said.

And then my mother said, "Joe"—that was the first time I had ever heard my mother call my father that—"when's the last time you brought me a prize?"

My father didn't say anything.

I kept the dice.

Sometime after the Blackfoot State Fair but before school started again, my mother finally got the window in the kitchen she had always wanted above the sink, so she could look out to the west while she washed the dishes. Before she'd had to look at the wall with a picture of the Last Supper on it.

My mother had talked about that window all that summer and the summer before, maybe even the summer before that. Forevermore is how long she had wanted that window, she said.

One morning at the breakfast table, my mother slammed down the plate of eggs and sausage and toast and hash-browns in front of my father and told him she was going to go find a bar and get drunk the next Saturday if she didn't have a window above the sink by then. My mother slammed his coffee cup down too, spilling coffee into his saucer, which was something my father hated.

My father ate his breakfast without saying a word. When it came time to drink his coffee, he poured what had spilled in the saucer back into the cup. He even got up himself and got the dish rag—didn't ask my mother or me to do it—and wiped off the bottom of the cup and then finished his coffee.

So, that Saturday, my grandfather—my father's father—came over, and my father and my grandfather, who was a carpenter, put the window in; at least my father tried to help my grandfather.

Everything started out fine. My father bought the window and got all the materials ready. My grandfather was supposed to come over Saturday afternoon, and he showed up, all right, but he was three hours late and real drunk. That's why my father had never tasted liquor, or so he claimed—I found out different later—but that's what my father told me: that he had never tasted liquor because his father was an alcoholic.

My mother said it different. She said that Grandpa Weber was a drunk, *an old drunk,* she said, a *damned old souse,* and when she called him that, she crossed herself.

When my grandfather started cutting a hole in the wall for a window, we all just left him alone. There was no use talking to him, trying to make sense to him, once he got a notion in his head when he was drunk like that.

That noise that electric saws make—that high-pitched loud sound that gets lower as it gets deeper into the wood—is what I remember about the kitchen window, that and my grandfather outside on the stepladder, sticking that blade into the side of the clapboard house, sawdust flying in his face, him cutting and cussing away. Didn't even measure, just walked up the ladder and stuck the blade into the house.

My father took off out of there fast, in the Oldsmobile, tires spinning and gravel spitting all over the place—he told my mother he was going irrigating—and my mother stood in the kitchen against the far wall and stared west, her hands on her ears, waiting for the blade to poke through the wall and praying for a miracle. Finally the saw blade poked through and as the hole got bigger, flies started coming in. Soon there were flies on everything; we couldn't hardly see the kitchen ceiling for flies. My mother crossed herself and went into her bedroom. She locked the door behind her and put a towel in the space under the door so the flies couldn't get in. Behind that door, I could hear her crying.

When my grandfather was done, I saw that the bottom of the hole he'd cut started at about my mother's chin; the glass part didn't start until her nose. She could see out, all right, but just barely. When she looked out, all she would see was sky.

The hole that my grandfather cut was too big for the window we'd bought to put in it, so my father spent the next day patching, even though it was Sunday and there wasn't supposed to be any servile work done. On the outside my mother painted my father's patch-up job white. Inside, she ended up repainting the whole kitchen, and later on that week she made a special trip to town. She bought some Virginia-creeper plants—one thing always leading to another—and planted those Virginia creepers and watered them every day for the rest of the summer to keep them from drying up. She trained them to crawl up the side of the house and around the window to cover up the eyesore, which is what my mother called it: *the eyesore. The old souse's eyesore,* she'd say, and cross herself.

So when that Saturday night came around, my mother didn't go find a bar and get drunk in it, and my father never said anything about her going to a bar, and he never said a thing about the eyesore. I never caught him so much as looking at it.

School was back on and I wasn't going to the St. Joseph's School anymore. I was going to the Hawthorne Junior High School and I didn't know anybody because everyone at Hawthorne was Mormon. I was Catholic, so I found I didn't like it there much at school. The worst—as usual—was physical education class, but I liked Miss Parkinson and my American history class.

She taught English, Miss Parkinson, and she wasn't a nun. She had blond curly hair that she stuck her pencil in, and when she talked to the class she would once in a while fluff up her curls, then shake them loose. She used to take a deep breath and pull her stomach in, and straighten out her dress under her belt. All the men teachers, especially Mr. Hoffman, the American history teacher, and Mr. Ashly, the science teacher, stopped by during home room to ask her things, like if she wanted coffee or if everything was all right. Mr. Hoffman, and sometimes Mr. Ashly, but never both of them at the same time, would stand outside in the hallway and when Miss Parkinson took a deep breath and pulled her chest up the way she did, and sucked in her stomach, you could see Mr. Hoffman or Mr. Ashly, depending on which one of them was out there in the hallway watching, take a deep breath too.

Miss Parkinson also taught speech third period. Once,

she had us give impromptu speeches. Each of us had to go up and stand in front of the whole class and give a speech on a topic that Miss Parkinson made up right then. I did terrible on the one she gave me: "Important Decisions I Have Made." I couldn't tell them about jumping in the river and all it led to. I really hadn't made any other decisions so I didn't have much to say. What I ended up saying was that I was glad that I decided to take speech class instead of Spanish class, but I couldn't say much more than that because right then I hated speech class.

Jimmy Terrel got the topic of beans. He recited a little poem about how beans give you gas and make you toot. Everybody laughed, even Miss Parkinson. I laughed so hard I had to leave the class. It was funny—farting always seemed funny to me then—and to talk about it in the class made it even funnier. It was too much. I told my mother how I had laughed in speech class and why. I told her Jimmy Terrel's poem and she laughed just about as hard as I had laughed, so then I went ahead and told her about the time that my father farted—my father was always farting loud when he wasn't around my mother—when he was fixing the hay rake one day. Our dog, Toby—this was before he died—was sitting right there under my father at the time. When my father farted so loud, Toby's ears perked up. He tilted his head a little to the side, sniffed, then got out of there real fast.

I had never seen my mother laugh so hard as when

I told her that story. I loved that she was laughing like that. That day, I decided I would try to make her laugh like that more often.

I'd studied American history at the St. Joseph's School, but those Holy Cross nuns didn't teach American history like Mr. Hoffman did at the Hawthorne Junior High School. He was old and smelled like cigarettes and his own self. He taught us that history was just a story that somebody was telling, and what happened in the story often depended on who was telling it. An *interpretation,* is what Mr. Hoffman always said that history was—like, for example, we think it was a good deal for us to buy Manhattan for twenty-four dollars in trinkets, but how do the Indians feel about that transaction? And Custer's Last Stand wasn't a massacre at all as far as the Indians are concerned. And how would you like it if the Ku Klux Klan hated you because of how *you* were? It was all a matter of *interpretation.*

Mr. Hoffman said that America was formed by people trying to get away so they could be how they were and exercise their right to their own interpretation and not be like governments and religions were saying they had to be.

It's a free country, is another thing Mr. Hoffman said over and over. *It's a free country.* I started saying that to myself, too: *It's a free country.*

I remember the day Mr. Hoffman first said that *history* was always just somebody's *interpretation* of the events, and not the events themselves. Sitting in Mr. Hoffman's class that day, I looked out the window and thought about what Mr. Energy had said at the Blackfoot State Fair, about everything being an illusion.

I spent a lot of time thinking about those two things, about *illusion* and *interpretation,* about the truth and stories about the truth, about reality and how things appear—and what I came up with was a headache.

The only thing I knew for sure was that it was a free country and that what both of those men were saying was that how things were, and how things seemed to be, were not always the same.

I got to be pretty good friends with Mr. Hoffman. Sometimes I would eat my lunch in his classroom and read *Time* magazine and we would talk. He gave me a book as a present. The name of it was *Manifest Destiny* and it was about American history—*a pretty good interpretation,* Mr. Hoffman had said.

There were three photographs in that book *Manifest Destiny* that I always used to look at. Sometimes at home, at night, when my mother and my father were asleep, I would turn on my light and look at those three pictures. One was a picture of Chief Joseph, not St. Joseph, *Chief* Joseph of the Nez Percé. I used to like to look at what he was wearing: beads and feathers that he had traded for Manhattan. His hair was long and braided. He had eyes that reminded me of the nigger's—of Geronimo's.

The second was the photograph of men dressed up in white sheets like priests, standing around a burning cross. In the background was a Negro man hanging.

The third photograph was of a big factory in Pittsburgh, Pennsylvania. There were big smokestacks with smoke and fire pouring out across the sky. The factory was made of tin as bright as the toolshed in the sun. Under the photograph was a chapter head: "The Industrial Revolution."

And something else different happened that year: at the end of September I received the sacrament of Holy Confirmation. I was late by a year—the year before, the bishop had been sick, and only the bishop could perform the sacrament of Holy Confirmation. My whole class at the St. Joseph's School had to wait till he was better.

Confirmation is the sacrament when the Holy Ghost comes down upon you. Once you're confirmed, you're grown-up in the eyes of the Church. To receive the sacrament you had to memorize the entire Baltimore catechism from cover to cover. You had to know it all, every page, because the bishop would ask you questions in front of the whole congregation about what was in that book. You never knew which one he was going to ask.

My mother bought me a suit for the occasion, a

second-hand one from the St. Joseph's Church rummage sale. She bought second-hand because I would just outgrow it. That suit was navy blue with wide lapels and awful baggy pants to match.

That Sunday, the Sunday of my Holy Confirmation, my mother and my father and I drove into town like usual, not saying much. We got to the church at eight-thirty and I told Monsignor Canby what I had done and how many times I had done it. Monsignor gave me a penance—five Our Fathers and five Hail Marys—and then I went up to sit with the rest of the confirmandees—that's what they called us: *confirmandees*. There were six of us and, as it ended up, the bishop only asked me one question. It was the second one in the book:

"If God is everywhere, why cannot we see Him?" the bishop wanted to know.

No problem. I stood up straight like I thought a saint would stand and imagined that a tongue of fire—the Holy Ghost—was coming down on me right then. I answered the question, my voice echoing in the nave. I answered like a grown-up Catholic: "We cannot see God because He is a Pure Spirit and cannot be seen with bodily eyes."

The bishop's sermon was about the Holy Trinity and how the Holy Trinity was a Divine Mystery: Three Beings in one and the same God: Father, Son, and Holy Ghost.

After Mass, in front of the church, my father took

my picture, with my mother behind him telling me how to smile so my crooked bottom teeth didn't show.

But being confirmed didn't change things as much as I'd hoped. It didn't stop any of those red flags, if you know what I mean. The only difference, as far as I could tell, was that I got a new name. I got to choose the name of the saint I most wanted to be like. From then on, it would be my confirmation name for the rest of my life.

I read *The Lives of the Saints* to help decide which saint to pick. Jacob was my given name, but the original Jacob was no saint; he wasn't even in the New Testament, let alone a Catholic.

One night, as the story goes, Jacob was just lying there in his bed when an archangel named Penuel descended and started wrestling with him. Jacob thought Penuel was a devil. All night they wrestled, breaking things and knocking things over, Penuel making that flapping sound with his wings. When morning came, Jacob had got the best of Penuel even though Penuel was an archangel. That's when Penuel told Jacob who he was. Jacob told Penuel he wouldn't let go until Penuel blessed him. Penuel had no choice. He gave Jacob his blessing.

In *The Lives of the Saints* I started reading about St. John Vianney. As soon as I read his story, I knew, he was the one: St. John Vianney, the Curé of Ars. I didn't know what that meant, "the Curé of Ars," but I chose him because he said he had wrestled with a devil, a real one. He was just lying there in his bed and a devil descended and St. John knew it was a devil right off. He wasn't fooled for a minute. I figured this St. John Vianney guy could help me out. He knew a devil when he wrestled with one. Plus he was a Catholic. So I chose him.

My confirmation certificate was written in that fancy kind of writing and it said that I had received the Sacrament of Holy Confirmation and that my confirmation name was John. I hung the certificate up on my bedroom wall next to the picture of the guardian angel helping the two little kids across the bridge.

I liked my new name a lot for about a week, but then, as it turned out, I never really got to use it. Everybody at the Hawthorne Junior High School was a Mormon so they wouldn't have understood about my new name, not that I ever talked to them much anyway. The only other people I talked to were my mother and my father and they didn't call me any name when they called to me. My father called me "lunkhead" now and then, so I just stuck to my regular name and Haji Baba when I was in the loft of the barn or up in the cottonwoods.

I still liked the story of Jacob and the Archangel Penuel and St. John Vianney and the devil going at it, though, and there were a couple of nights I woke up ready for a fight, but I was alone.

I saw the nigger two more times before I saw him hanging there from the winch in the back of the barn, strung up with the ropes of my swing, although I really didn't see the nigger the first of these two times.

The Matisse County Mounted Posse hadn't been around for some time, and the nigger's lean-to looked no different from the first few times that they had ransacked it—the window was still broken, the back door was open, and there was stuff strewn all over the backyard, busted up. I figured the Matisse County Mounted Posse had long since given up on the nigger since I hadn't seen them around for so long. One evening I heard my father tell my mother that the sheriff had told him that the nigger had probably hopped a freight and gone south—back to his own kind. "Or joined the circus," I said aloud in the hallway of the butterflies and dice when I heard my father tell my mother about the nigger jumping a freight. Ever since I heard that that's what the sheriff thought, that the nigger had jumped a freight, I would say, *Geronimo and Haji Baba jumped a freight;* it got to be a chant, *joined the circus. Geronimo and Haji Baba jumped a freight, joined the circus, a freight for Nantucket, Oshkosh, Timbuktu;* I'd say it to myself over and over again while I was ticking off the red flags, while I was swinging, shooting for sunset, and a bull's-eye.

It was a Saturday the first time I saw the nigger. That was the time I just knew that he was there. I'm sure it was a Saturday because there wasn't any school that day and it wasn't Sunday because we didn't go to church that day. It was Saturday in the late afternoon. The sky was golden, the way it gets that time of year, that time of day. There was a steady wind and you could hear things from a long way off. I was sitting by the narrow, fast place in the river—my father called them the Popcorn Fart Falls because the river was so low that year—in a sunny spot.

An orange peel shaped like a heart floated over the falls and down, and then an orange peel shaped like a diamond floated over and down, and then an orange peel shaped like a four-leaf clover floated by; finally an orange peel shaped like a spade floated over the falls and vanished. I turned to look upstream and saw a beautiful boat floating down the river, a barge. It looked Egyptian—like something Cleopatra would have to float down the river. The boat was made from a pod from the catalpa tree, and in the pod, in the boat, there was a layer of orange-peel carpet and trees made out of sticks with orange-peel tops. There were hollyhock ladies in full hollyhock skirts and wide-brimmed hollyhock hats. There were magical animals made from tinfoil that stood around the hollyhock ladies under the orange-peel trees, and there were orange-carpeted steps that went up to an altar.

There was a photograph of her there, of that woman Sugar Babe.

But the photograph looked like a lot of women I knew. The photograph looked like Cleopatra, like Hedy Lamarr, like the woman in the ticket booth at the

Blackfoot State Fair; the photograph looked like the Virgin Mary, like my mother.

Around the photograph of that woman was a frame of ribbons and feathers and the beads that bought Manhattan and little white flowers and pieces of sagebrush and silver leaves from the cottonwood trees.

All around the photograph there were dollar bills that stuck out from the frame, dollar bills pinned to the photograph; pinned to the altar; dollar bills everywhere, sticking out from the orange-peel carpet and the orange-peel trees. Some of the magic animals stood on dollars.

I had never seen so much money, ever.

I did not touch a thing, not a dollar, not a flower. In fact, I moved back out of the river and sat myself down on the lava rock and pulled my knees up. I watched as the barge went over the falls, slowly. There wasn't much current. I sat in the niche of the lava rock in a sunny place that the wind passed by and the sky didn't get to, and watched the barge as it went over. It went down fast and rammed into a rock. The pod split, the orange trees fell into the river, the hollyhock ladies in their hollyhock hats flew overboard, the magic animals went over the side, their shiny foil sinking into darkness. The dollar bills, the flowers, the beads, and the ribbons went down. The picture sank. Nothing floated back up.

I sat and watched the water there for a long time. I sat there until way past suppertime and thought about things, one thought leading to another, but mostly leading to the nigger, to Geronimo, all the time the sky getting bigger and darker. There were two butterflies on the grass just sitting there, not flying, though their wings were still going. A green-and-blue dragonfly shined in the twilight as though it held sun from the day. Hawks glided past between me and the moon, just hanging up there, glowing.

After a while, I got up and looked for the nigger, but not very hard. I knew I wouldn't find him.

I went back to that spot the next day—Sunday after the red flags, confession, and Mass, after breakfast and the chores, and sat there again in the sunny place all day. There was no sign of the nigger, but I came back a week later, on the next Saturday. Still there was no sign of him.

But I did see something else that day. I didn't see the nigger, but I saw Harold P. Endicott.

I wandered downstream because the wind was snapping Harold P. Endicott's big American flag and it got to be an itch, that flag. Old Glory snapping was an itch I just had to scratch.

I waded downstream and really didn't let myself know that I was going to Harold P. Endicott's. I just spent my time looking at things in the river and on the banks—trees, rocks, water skippers—that flag calling me over there the whole time, snapping for my attention, and I followed, taking my time, stopping and going with no apparent destination, though really I had a very definite one.

I climbed up an elm tree on our side of the river and sat there on a big limb pretending not to be where I was because Harold P. Endicott's big old haunted house was right there in front of me, just across the river, the cool dark grass of his back lawn sloping up to the stone castle walls. And above the haunted castle, above it all, was Old Glory, right there in front of me.

I was thinking about America, all those new things I was learning about America—Manifest Destiny, Inalienable Rights, and the Pursuit of Happiness—when all of a sudden Harold P. Endicott himself came out the back door of his house—the *second time* I had seen him walk out the back of a house that way—but this time he wasn't hitting any woman. He stepped out of the shade, into the sun, and stretched. He looked around, then blew on the whistle that hung around his neck. In seconds he was surrounded by his hellhounds.

When I saw those hellhounds come running around the house, believe me, I wished I wasn't there. I cussed myself good for getting so close to one of those forbidden people, but mostly so close to those hellhounds that could probably smell me. I got that deep feeling in me like I had to go to the bathroom, that fear feeling, and I started to move, so slow I felt like I wasn't even moving. I made it from the middle of that branch to the trunk of the tree, and when I got to the trunk, I made myself just another limb and I made myself smell like the tree.

Harold P. Endicott played around with his dogs, roughousing with them. Then he threw sticks into the river for them to fetch. One time, one of those hellhounds was right below me under the tree, looking for the stick that Endicott had thrown there. I breathed tree and tried to grow elm leaves. But after a while, after I watched him playing with his dogs, Harold P. Endicott just seemed like any other old man in his backyard, having fun with his dogs, no problem; running back and forth on the lawn with his dogs at his heels in the afternoon.

Old Endicott sat down on the grass then; I could see that he was breathing hard. He took his hat off and wiped his head. Then he took his boots off, and his socks, stuffing the socks into his boots as he lay down. His hellhounds surrounded him in a perfect order, like they had been trained to be at those places: one dog at his head, a dog on each side of him, and two dogs at his feet. The two dogs at his feet started licking his feet and in between his toes. The dog at his head started licking his bald head and neck and ears. Harold P. Endicott sat up and looked around and then undid his shirt. The two dogs on each side of him started licking his belly and up his sides. Endicott raised his arms and the dogs licked under his arms. Endicott kind of squirmed when those two dogs got under his arms. He sat up and looked around again and then undid his

Levi's, pulled them off, and his shorts too. He took off his shirt and stuck his shorts inside his Levi's. Then all he had on was his whistle. Then those two dogs started licking him down there, up his legs from his feet; the two dogs at his sides licking him down from his arms to below his belly, then down to as far as the other two dogs were licking up. All of those dogs went on that way for quite some time, and then Harold P. Endicott rolled over onto his stomach—because one thing always leads to another, I guess—and the dogs kept licking him from their assigned positions. At one point, Harold P. Endicott got up and knelt. He bent over and the two dogs at his feet went to him and licked him back in there while the other dogs sat back obediently and watched.

"Lard Ass," I whispered, and wanted to laugh, but didn't. I didn't move.

Old Harold P. Endicott stayed that way for quite some time, his ear to the ground, not looking around, kind of moving back and forth, like the screen door the night of the chinook, between here and there, just letting himself go, when all of a sudden he rolled over onto his side and the dogs stopped. He lay like that for a while, covering himself down there with his hands, and then, as if he had blown the whistle, those dogs started licking him all over again in the same way, from their same positions: the two on the sides going down and the two at his feet coming up, and then all of them there, in the middle, licking.

After a while, Harold P. Endicott got up and walked

back up to the house, naked except for his whistle. One of those dogs got his boots with his socks stuffed in them, and one of those dogs got his Levi's with his shorts stuffed in them, and another dog got his shirt, another his hat, and the five of those hellhounds followed him back into the house, the big stone haunted castle house in the trees, under the snapping flag, under Old Glory up there in the wind in the sky. I held on tight to the tree to keep from falling: off the tree, off the round ball that was turning at an illusive speed, off the round ball hanging there in infinity, in eternity, in the sky. Endicott closed the door, snugged it back into home. I heard the door shut just as Endicott closed it. I wasn't that far away.

The night she shot the moon, the moon was almost full and it was Saturday night, but it was different that night from most Saturday nights because my mother and my father had stayed in all day with the bills. There were bills and papers all over the kitchen table, from here to kingdom come on the kitchen table. *Settling-up time,* my father called it, and my mother called it *time when the vultures get their claws in you*. Both of them were acting like they acted when they were mad at each other at the Blackfoot State Fair, but during bill time they just seemed like they were mad at each other. Really they weren't.

The both of them sat there all day at the kitchen table frowning and my father cussing under his breath and making his knuckles white and my mother smoking his Viceroys, her voice lower, his higher, scratching numbers onto papers and putting papers into piles and then moving those piles to other piles, and then starting all over again, looking under piles for other papers, but what they were looking for was more money and it was never there.

There was so much paper on the kitchen table that there wasn't room to eat dinner, and dinner turned out to be only bologna sandwiches and fried spuds.

By suppertime they had managed to clear most of the bills and the papers away, most of them, that is, except for one, the big one, the farm payment, the one they only had half of. No matter how much they figured and scratched around and looked under piles and moved papers from one pile to another pile, they could only come up with half.

Endicott's bill sat on the supper table like something that shouldn't be among our things—like Montgomery Clift's martini glass might seem if it were sitting there. My father picked the bill up a couple of times and looked at it and then looked at his checkbook again, then laid the biil back down on the table, turned it over, picked it up again, then put it back down.

We ate supper with that piece of paper that night like it was a person there with us, like Old Lard Ass himself. I had half a mind to set a place for that bill: a knife and fork and spoon, bologna sandwich and spuds.

Nobody said anything during supper. Usually that was the case at supper—none of us saying much. Usually there wasn't much to say. But that night, that Saturday night, things were different because of that paper sitting there across from me, different because we only had half of what that paper said we had to have, like company with bad manners asking for more. That, to me, was something to talk about, but we didn't talk. It wasn't just that they weren't talking to me about it; they weren't talking to each other about it either.

I figured I would be different too: I wasn't going to be nice, start saying nice things about how things were happening, how good the bologna sandwiches were and the spuds, and what a nice pink color Old Lard Ass's bill was, but I was scared the way I get when things get like that—my mother and my father so quiet. I was more scared than usual this time, so much going on and nobody saying anything about it, the both of them acting like everything was normal, ordinary, that there was nothing wrong.

That always makes me scared—their acting—but this time it felt like it was just going to be too much. Too much for all of us, my mother, my father, and me. And we sat there like my mother's pressure cooker on the stove; the dial going up and up and we were just sitting there in a pressure cooker. The dial goes past all the numbers and starts going around again, like on the swing when you go so high the swing starts going over onto itself.

And so I said, "Pinochle. How about a game of pinochle?" I said to both of them, but really just to my mother so my father could hear, because he usually only played pinochle when there were four, when company came over and there were four. When it was just my mother, my father, and me, there had to be three extra cards called the widow so just the three of us could play.

"We'll see," my mother said, which usually meant no. "We'll see after the dishes are done," she told me. "And after the baths."

We only took baths on Saturday and we all used to share the same tub of water—me first, then my mother, and then my father—until I started getting older two years ago. Then I got my own tub of water, but usually I went first still.

I turned on KSEI on the radio while my mother and I did the dishes and my father sat at the supper table with his coffee and Endicott's pink bill. The sky through the eyesore was the color of blue that skies get in movies—Technicolor ones—and the Sons of the Pioneers were singing on the radio, "Cool Water," and then there was that dance kind of music like people used to dance to—Benny Goodman and Glenn Miller.

I'll be down to getcha in a taxi, honey,
better be ready 'bout half-past eight.

I asked my mother how you fox-trot.

My mother looked at me like she knew what I was doing—making things nice—and her look was a good one, one that said *thank you, I'm glad you're still trying to make things nice,* and she took her hands out of the dishwater and shook them off and dried them with a dish towel. My mother walked up to me and put my left hand on her right shoulder and my right hand on her waist and she told me to make a box with my feet, *make a box,* she said, *one, two, three, four,* she said. But she told me I was *two left feet.* Then she said, *Come on, Dad, let's show our son here how to fox-trot.* And sure enough, my father got up and took a hold of her. He kind of leaned down a bit to her and she raised her shoulders like she had shoulder pads on and they fox-trotted, all around the room, all around the supper table they fox-trotted, making boxes *one, two, three, four,* like Montgomery Clift and Hedy Lamarr, around that piece of pink paper on the supper table, my mother smiling on her tiptoes like she was wearing her high heels with no toes in them, and my father with a romantic look on his face, making that romantic look so I could see it, my father dancing and looking that way.

And then we took our baths, me first, them still fox-trotting. I could hear them there in the kitchen. I watched myself in the mirror of the medicine cabinet, listening to them in the kitchen, and then I smelled the coffee from the percolator and when my mother got done with her bath, and my father got done with his, we played pinochle. I had coffee too—in the special cups that matched the saucers—and chocolate cake, and my mother shot the moon in hearts, just exactly the right cards in the widow for a family.

And when I was in bed later, she came in and stood over me. She touched the covers and then walked to the window and looked out at the moon—the almost full moon she had just shot—and she said, "Good night." I had to agree. Even with Endicott's bill there, it had been a good one.

The next morning, when we got up, the hawks were back in the poplars in front of the house. As soon as my mother saw them through the front-room window, she crossed herself and went for her rosary.

On October 22 my father put his Sunday suit on even though it was a Monday, gassed up the Oldsmobile, and drove into town smelling like Old Spice. He drove to Harold P. Endicott's Bank and Trust on Main Street and Jefferson in Wind River with only half the farm payment. Then he drove back home with the news that we had to leave because we had lost the farm for good.

I was in the loft of the barn scaring up pigeons when I heard the Oldsmobile drive into the yard, heard him shut the engine off, heard him slam the door of the Oldsmobile. I heard the screen door slam next, which I expected, but then I heard him yell something and the screen door slam again and then I heard my father below me unlocking the saddle-room door. I got down onto the floor quick where there was a hole in the floorboards and I could see my father at the saddle-room door in his Sunday suit unlocking the saddle-room door with his right hand. In his left hand were two bottles of whiskey. At least I thought it was whiskey in those bottles, and as it turned out it was. It was Black Velvet, and when he got that saddle-room door unlocked, my father walked in there and closed the door behind him, locked it, and started drinking that Black Velvet down. He didn't come out at six for supper, and as things turned out, he finished up both of those Black Velvets by suppertime at six o'clock the next day.

In the kitchen at suppertime that first night, my mother put the food on the table, the roast beef and the mashed potatoes, and the string beans and the coleslaw and the bread, and the gravy. She even started the coffee up for my father for after supper, her hair the way she always combed it out for him at suppertime, her lips with lipstick on them, the clean apron she wore over her red housedress on, but my father didn't come in for supper still.

My mother stood at the kitchen window, the good one that faced out into the yard with the doily curtain and the red geranium in it, ready for him like that, her left hand drawing back the curtain, the hand with the wedding ring on it. My mother waited and the light changed from day—blue and yellow—through the colors of the rose window at church: orange and light red, navy blue to black. My mother waited until nighttime. When darkness fell, the light went on in the saddle-room and you could hear my father singing, *"Du, du liegst mir im Herzen,"* the waxing moon, even fuller than the night my mother'd shot it, rising over the ridgepole of the barn.

There were big white fluffy clouds going over the moon, white like the moon, when the saddle-room light finally went off. It wasn't long before I could see my father walking across the yard like he was trying to walk normal. I watched him from my window upstairs.

I wondered if my father could see us—his wife and his son at the windows, her down in the kitchen and me in my bedroom. If my father could see us, I wondered what he thought of us then. Then I wondered what it felt like for him to see us watching him walk like that.

My mother came into my room like she had two nights before after shooting the moon, but this night it was different, that left eye of hers was so far gone it looked like the eye of a fish dead and floating in a fish bowl. My mother pulled the covers of my bed back and fluffed the pillow up and stood there waiting for me to get into bed like I was still a kid. I already had my pajamas on, and she said that I could brush my teeth in the morning. I got in bed and my mother pulled the covers over me like I was still a kid and she stood there for a while in the dark in the moonlight. From downstairs we heard my father open the door. We heard the screen-door spring stretching. That night the screen door spring stretching like that sounded like angels singing, glorious and sorrowful both.

"Looks like we've lost the farm for good," my mother said, and I didn't say anything.

"Whatever happens tonight," she said, "I don't want you coming out of your room. There's trouble enough without you two getting into it. Promise me," she said, and I promised.

My mother left the room then and closed the door behind her and there was only darkness, save for the moonlight in the room. I could hardly make out my confirmation certificate and the picture of the guardian angel helping the two kids across the bridge.

Pretty soon I could hear them talking in the kitchen, my mother talking like she was whispering, though she wasn't, my father talking loud in the way I had never heard him talk in front of her before, saying those words in front of her and in a strange voice—a drunken voice, I figured—and the both of them were calling each other *Joe* and *Mary*. Later on, I could hear my father puking in the bathroom and then later I could hear my mother crying in the bedroom.

In the morning, I didn't go to school. Nobody even

thought of it, including me. My father still had his suit on. He was sitting in the front room in the early-morning light that was the color of eggshells. There he was: in his suit, on the davenport like he was company, holding on to the second Black Velvet. The first Black Velvet was in the kitchen on the draining board. My mother had rinsed it out.

When I saw my father sitting there in his Sunday suit in that light holding on to the Black Velvet that way, and my mother wearing lipstick and her hair the way she wore it for him, and nobody even thinking about getting me to school, I got scared in a way I had never been scared before.

My father sat there in the front room through breakfast, passing up on the mush, the eggs fried just the way he liked them, and the toast. He didn't even have any coffee.

My father sat there through dinner, passing up on the roast beef from the night before when he didn't eat supper, the potatoes, the gravy, the string beans—reheated; the coleslaw, the baked bread, the peach pie—his favorite—and coffee again.

Even though it was Tuesday, my mother didn't bake bread. She didn't do the ironing. She just sat at the kitchen table smoking Viceroys, waiting for my father to eat.

My father sat there drinking from the second bottle of Black Velvet all through supper—no roast-beef sandwiches, no potato salad, no corn on the cob, no peach pie, still no coffee for him.

But then, just about the time that supper was usually over, my father stood up and drained the last of the Black Velvet from the bottle and let the bottle fall to the floor on the carpet. Just about the time my father usually took his paper into the front room or out on the front porch with his coffee, my father walked down the hallway of the butterflies and dice. He walked into the kitchen and my mother was waiting for him with the rolling pin. My mother was in the kitchen with her hair that way for him, lipstick on her lips for him, wearing her clean apron over her red housedress for him, with her rolling pin in her hand for him. When my father stepped into the kitchen, my mother unlatched and came on him fast from behind from where she had been standing. She swung a good one but missed him by a yard, lost her balance and fell down by the stove, her hair falling down in front of her eyes, her dress up, her legs bare all the way up to her panties. My mother stood up again real fast and cranked up for another swing, but my father stopped her, hit her in the mouth with his fist clenched tight. He hit her the way one man hits another man in a fistfight or boxing; the way Harold P. Endicott hit that woman Sugar Babe. My mother's nose and mouth went red and she went down fast into the pile of kindling by the stove.

My father hit me the same way when I went after him. I heard a loud buzzing and I felt like puking. I landed on top of my mother by the stove. My father said something about the way the two of us, my mother and me, were lying there, and then walked out the kitchen door, slamming the screen door behind him as he left.

I just lay there for a while looking at things. I had never seen the kitchen door from that angle. Looking out the eyesore from down there, I saw more sky than I'd ever seen from inside before. Then one of those hawks flew by—framed for an instant by the eyesore. That bird let out a screech that was just like the screen-door spring stretching. I don't know how I ever could have thought it sounded like angels.

I looked over at my mother. Her eyes were open and she was staring up at the ceiling, holding her hand over her nose and mouth. Her eye was worse than ever. It was like she had finally seen too much. I got up and got a washrag wet and gave it to her and she began to wipe the blood away.

"Go after your father," my mother said. "He needs you now." And after she said that, she crossed herself. Then she got up and walked into the hallway of the butterflies and the dice and into the bathroom and closed the door behind her.

The door to the saddle room was open and where the .25-20 usually hung was just the red outline on the wall. I ran to the river to old Harold P. Endicott's house. Everything along the way looked like that missing rifle; things were just outlines of themselves—the barn, the house, the toolshed, the trees, the pig pen, the river, even the clouds. As I ran I wondered why I was thinking that things looked that way. I figured it was because I was scared. Things always seemed different then. But I never stopped running, scared as I was. I never stopped even when the rain started. Even when the skies grew black and opened up. I never stopped until I got to Harold P. Endicott's, where Old Lard Ass had got his licking; never stopped until I heard the shot.

This is what I saw: my father holding the gun on Harold P. Endicott, who was sitting in a lawn chair under the eaves of his house near the back door, his hellhounds surrounding him, all of them looking at my father like murder. I don't know why, but I was relieved for all of us that my father didn't catch old Endicott like I had caught him that day.

My father was standing there in the rain, holding the gun on Harold P. Endicott. He had Harold P. Endicott in his sights; he was looking down the barrel at him, at Endicott's round, bald head. A bull's-eye. My father was talking but I couldn't hear the words, so I ducked down and ran through the brush, up to a big weeping willow. I hid behind it.

"The next shot is between your eyes, Mr. Big Shot, unless you get those dogs inside," I heard my father say in his drunken voice.

Harold P. Endicott looked at his hellhounds, that

whistle dangling from his neck. Their ears were perked up and they stared at their master without moving a muscle, not one.

"And don't try anything funny. I know all about how you like to kill people with those dogs of yours. Just killed you a Bannock squaw, didn't you?" my father said.

Old Endicott got real stiff, as stiff as his dogs; then he stood up fast and my father cocked the .25-20 and shot it, hitting the stone wall behind Endicott. Pieces of stone sprayed out and Endicott sat back down. Those hellhounds didn't flinch, but you could tell they were slobbering to kill.

"Don't press me, you crooked son of a bitch!" my father said. "I've killed me a bunch of people in my time and I sure as hell can kill one more if it's you!"

Harold P. Endicott snapped his fingers and stood up, slow this time, walked to the back door and opened it, never turning his back on my father's gun. He closed the door behind the dogs after they filed inside, one by one.

I heard my father say, "Pull the door tight and lock it!"

I ran around to the front of the house because I knew the front door was going to be open, and sure enough it was. I ran to the door, Old Glory there snapping loud above me, and I pulled the front door closed just as the first of the dogs got to it, murder only inches away.

I leaned up against the house for a while, so much

sky in my lungs I thought I was going to float away, but then I ran to the back again, hoping there weren't any other doors or windows open too. When I got back to the back of the house, I couldn't believe my eyes.

My father had taken his suit jacket off and was rolling up his shirt sleeves. He had his chest puffed out and was muttering something, rolling up his sleeves.

"A fair fight," my father said. "Like a man," my father said.

"Where's the gun?" I said, but my father didn't hear me. Harold P. Endicott didn't hear me either; the rain had started down hard.

Harold P. Endicott took his hat off and took a few steps, his whistle bouncing against his chest. He and my father squared off, fists out in front of them. Endicott hit my father in the mouth and my father went flying like my mother had when my father hit her earlier that night. Endicott laughed and took a step back. My father sat in the wet grass, shaking his head and holding his jaw. Then my father stood up and Endicott hit him again, but my father didn't go down this time. My father came back with a punch in Endicott's mouth, then one in Endicott's big stomach. Then my father kicked him between the legs and Endicott doubled up, his nose bleeding, and held himself down there. I let out a cheer but I don't think either of them heard; the rain was coming down loud as the river.

My father dropped his arms and looked up into the

sky like it was the first time that he realized that it was raining. He put his face into the rain the way my mother had stood herself into that wind the night of the chinook. As my father was looking up, Endicott hit him in the stomach, hard, swinging his arm into my father like a baseball bat. My father went sprawling out onto the grass, spread-eagled. He was out like a light, KO'd. Endicott kicked my father in the stomach the way I'd seen him kick that woman Sugar Babe. My father let out an awful sound—a sound like water going down the drain. After that, he didn't move.

It was then I saw it, the .25-20. It was propped against a pile of bricks at the edge of the lawn. Endicott started to turn back to the house, holding up the whistle with his hand. I ran to the rifle, picked it up, and aimed at Endicott's head. Endicott had the whistle in his mouth. He was almost to the door. The cross inside the sights of the .25-20 was between his right eye and his ear. I pulled the trigger but nothing happened.

Endicott's hand was on the knob, turning.

I cocked the rifle and the cross was right on the back of his head, just above the larded wrinkle. Then he turned around. Endicott had heard me cock the rifle. He turned around and looked straight at me—the cross was on his forehead. He looked me in the eye, that whistle of his in his mouth.

"Forevermore," I said.

His eyes locked on mine, squinting down the sights. I set the cross on his left eye. Soon as I did, his eye changed. An arrow pierced it. Then his right eye wasn't there either; it looked off into the distance. Endicott stepped back, the whistle fell from his mouth, then his knees gave way. He knelt for a moment, then fell forward. His ear was to the ground again, the way I'd seen him the other day, and his lard ass in the air.

Geronimo was standing on the lawn, just at the edge of the river, bow drawn, eyes fierce like a hawk's, like a snake's. He was naked except for a string around his waist with a patch of leather that hung down in front of him. There were beads on it—the beads that bought Manhattan—and a hunting knife in a sheath hanging from the string. Around his neck was a necklace with beads the color of the sky at night. Geronimo's face and the right side of his body were covered with designs in muddy red paint—designs like you might see on rattlesnakes, or maybe butterflies. He did not move for some time. He just stood there pointing at Endicott lying there with his ear to the ground, pointing out Endicott's death to the world.

I did not know how to uncock the rifle—my father had never shown me, not that I'd wanted to learn—so I pointed the .25-20 at the grass and pulled the trigger. The sound of the blast echoed through the trees and went up the river and down the river and up into the sky. After that it was quiet except for the rain. Then I heard another sound like children crying or lots of people way far away cheering—I couldn't tell which—but then I knew that the sound was coming from Geronimo. He had started to sing the kinds of songs Indians sing—songs that are like animal sounds.

Geronimo started to move toward his prey then, laying his bow down gently. His step was more like dancing than a walk, and he was still singing as he went. Geronimo bent over and smelled Endicott like a dog would smell him. Then he circled around him again and again, dancing and singing the whole while.

Geronimo placed his foot on Endicott's mouth and pulled the arrow from his eye. *Heya, heya, heya,* Geronimo sang. Then he made a crying sound, then a howling dog sound. He pulled the whistle from Endicott's neck and held it up to the sky along with the arrow, like he was showing the sky, showing God, that Geronimo had gotten the whistle, finally. *Heya, heya, heya, I got the whistle.* And then Geronimo put the whistle around his own neck.

Geronimo took the knife out of its sheath and showed the blade to the sky, like he was telling the story as he was living it.

As I watched, I realized he wasn't really a nigger. He was an Indian, like Sugar Babe. But then, watching him there in the rain like that, watching him like he was, I decided he was just himself, pure and simple: a person, like me. He was Geronimo being himself in our free country.

Geronimo brought the knife down and sliced part of Endicott's head off, sliced along that lard wrinkle in the back. He took Endicott's scalp and raised it up; showed it to the sky and told the story. Then he put the knife back into his sheath and picked up the arrow that had pierced Endicott's eye. Geronimo picked up another arrow that was lashed to the bow and took those two arrows and made a cross with them. He raised that cross up in his left hand; in his right hand was Endicott's scalp. Geronimo walked to the river slowly, dancing to his own wild animal sounds. He waded in up to his knees, letting the blood drip into the river. Geronimo told his story to the river too. Then he turned and told it to the east, then to the south, to the west, and finally to the north. *Heya, heya, heya,* he sang, *heya, heya, Sugar Babe,* he sang, *heya, heya, Sugar Babe.*

I went back around to the front door like Geronimo told me and got the hellhounds' attention by opening the door an inch, then closing it again. I did it over and over, while Geronimo took Endicott's clothes off his body like he told me he was going to do. Geronimo dragged Endicott into the house through the back door and laid him down there on the front-room floor in front of the fireplace. He put Endicott's clothes in a pile next to him, shorts stuffed in the Levi's, socks stuffed in the boots, just the way Endicott had done it. Geronimo smiled to me and said, *you know, just like usual.* When I got the signal that said the coast was clear, I closed the door for good, wiping the fingerprints off the knob just in case.

Then I took Old Glory down like Geronimo told me to do and folded it up like I had for flag duty at the St. Joseph's School. I brought that flag to him like he said.

Geronimo looked at Old Glory all folded up proper like that and laughed. He took it from me and shook it out the way my mother shakes out the tablecloth. He laid that American flag down next to my father. Together we rolled my father into it. My father wasn't dead, just dead drunk. Geronimo could tell the difference.

I cleaned the stone chips off the ground from when my father'd shot the wall. Geronimo picked up his bow and arrows. I got the .25-20, and my father's suit jacket. Geronimo found the three empty bullet shells. He got the blood up from the grass where Endicott had been. I don't know how Geronimo took away that stain, but he did. I looked around a final time; there was no trace of what had happened.

Geronimo said it was important to get out of there before the rain stopped. It was about ready to let up, he said. We were about to pick my father up on the red-white-and-blue stretcher—get out of there for good—when Geronimo walked back up to the house. I wish I hadn't followed him back there, but I did.

We looked in the window.

Those five hellhounds were sitting around Endicott in their assigned positions, licking away like I saw them do before. The dog at Endicott's head was licking at his scalped place. He was biting at it too.

I helped Geronimo carry my father down the road a piece, but then I felt like I was going to puke and then I did start puking. I began to see only the outlines of things again; everything was traced like the things back in my father's saddle room. I started shaking all over, the fear that was always in me finally coming out. I tried to stop shaking, but couldn't. I looked around. Everything seemed like the sound of the screen door when you were far away from it. I went down fast, flat as a pancake on the flat cookie sheet of earth. It was all I could do to keep from falling off the planet. I looked above me; all I could see was sky.

I remember thinking that the rain hadn't stopped, and I was glad it hadn't. The last thing I remember before I finally did fall into infinity, before I woke up in that room in the St. Anthony's Hospital, was Geronimo carrying me and singing. But this time his song wasn't a howl or a cry. His song was the kind that made you want to sleep, maybe forever. Maybe forevermore.

The nurse said *over a week now,* and then she said *fever* and then she said *vivid imagination.* My mother came in and crossed herself. Her one eye was still looking far off and it was black and blue.

When the nurse was gone my mother said *American flag* and *sober* and *I love you.* She left when my father came in. My father stayed but didn't say anything, not until the sheriff came. The sheriff said *pile of bones* and *nigger* and *scalp* and *whistle.*

I stayed at the bottom of the river with the photograph of that woman Sugar Babe, with the dollar bills and the beads there in that room in the St. Anthony's Hospital. When I knew the time was right, I pulled those underwater tubes out of my nose. I got up and checked the door a couple of times, opening it up an inch and then closing it over and over again, like I'd done that night, the way Geronimo had told me. Those hell-hounds were trying to get in. I shut the door tight and crawled out the window; slid down the eave to the trellis with the Seven Sister rose hanging from it. I hopped a freight and joined the circus a thousand times. Mainly, I got myself out of that room in the St. Anthony's Hospital. Haji Baba and Geronimo joined the circus together, hopped a freight. Everything was an illusion, from Nantucket to Oshkosh to Timbuktu to Broadway. Haji Baba and Geronimo swinging high, the swing going over onto itself, back to where things were normal again. Sprung back into home. Snug with American history, roast beef and spuds, farts, one thing leading to another, no problem forevermore.

The Indians parked in the back alley behind the Working Man's Club gave me a ride most of the way to the farm. They gave me a beer, a Rainier, and I sat in the front seat, riding shotgun by the window. Next to me was a woman named Mona Lisa who sat between me and the driver eating boiled eggs.

Wolf, the man who was driving, asked me if I had any money for gas. I said no, I didn't, and then somebody else in there, some woman, said *what can you do for us then?* And all of them laughed. *He's got a big trinket for you,* one of them said, and then they all laughed again. Somebody said *sing for his supper* and there was more laughter, and when they quit laughing, Wolf said *you got any trinkets?* and I said *the trinkets that bought Manhattan,* and for some reason they all laughed again. I didn't think what I said was funny. I wondered how they could think it was. Finally I told them I could sing and dance.

They really laughed at that, the Studebaker bouncing up and down. *Elvis Presley,* someone said. *No, Pat Boone,* said someone else. *Marge and Gower Champion,* said someone. *Tennessee Ernie Ford, Sixteen tons and what do you get,* someone said, and everybody sang, *another day older and deeper in debt,* together, like they had been practicing that song for years. Then they all laughed again, but it got quiet when I started.

I started dancing the way animals move, the way birds fly up, the way the chinook blew. I danced the way Geronimo danced, the way rattlesnakes move, the way dogs sniff the air. I told my story the way Geronimo told his story that night. I sang the *heya, heya, heya, Sugar Babe* song, the *heya, heya, Geronimo and Haji Baba jumped a freight, joined the circus, shooting the moon* song; the *Holy Ghost got you* song, the *wrestling with an angel* song, the *long-lost friend* song, the *flat-as-a-cookie-sheet* and the *sky-infinity* song. Old Glory. *Oh beautiful for spacious skies.*

When I got done, there was no laughter coming out of the Studebaker. There were no sounds to fill up the space where the sound of my song had been.

Wolf turned around to Mona Lisa and she cracked an egg on the dashboard and peeled it, shells falling into her lap. They all talked to each other in their language, a language Geronimo would know. It sounded like arguing, but Mona Lisa scooted over closer to Wolf and said something real loud. Everybody listened to Mona Lisa and it got quiet again.

Wolf turned back around to me and said, *you can ride with us if you don't mind getting a DWI.* I told Wolf that I didn't know what that was, a DWI.

Drunk with Indians, he said, and then the Studebaker started bouncing up and down again, and it wasn't quiet there anymore, all of them laughing again. Then Mona Lisa said, *give him a beer.*

Wolf stopped the car at the place where the main highway to town meets with the Portneuf River to let me out. They were going on to Fort Hall.

I stood there on the flat dusty road, the moon waning and the dome above me poked with star-holes. I watched until the Studebaker's taillights dipped into the dark sky. Then I followed the river downstream. I ran into some bats, so I started walking alongside the river, out away from the trees. When I got to where the river dog-legs, by my secret place in the stand of the twenty-two cottonwood trees, I saw that somebody had cut down my swing.

I decided to go home.

The Oldsmobile wasn't there and the house was dark. I walked inside. No one was there and some things were missing: my mother's rosary, her prayer book, her lipstick, and her high heels with the holes in the toes, my father's Old Spice, the toothbrushes, the percolator, and the radio. There was some peach pie in the refrigerator and milk gone sour, but no Black Velvet whiskey bottles. Everything else—the davenport and the coffee table, my father's chair, the beds, and the kitchen table and chairs—was all there. The geranium in the window was dead and things weren't cleaned up so much like usual.

I thought for a minute that I might still be dreaming. Everything seemed underwater, like when I was down in the bottom of that pool with the picture of that woman Sugar Babe. I went through the hallway and touched all the butterflies and all the dice. Then I went into the bathroom and looked into the medicine-cabinet mirror and watched myself touch my face, then touch my reflection in the mirror. Everything felt real, or seemed real enough, and I thought back to that magician guy, Mr. Energy, and all he'd said.

In the yard, there wasn't any tractor or hay baler or drain grill, or disc and harrows parked around. I stopped at the saddle-room door and tried the knob. It was still locked. I couldn't see in, but I could tell that things were the same in there. By the smell and by the way the floor was swept clean, I knew.

I walked out the back door of the barn to see if the holsteins were in the back corral and if the pigs were in their pen. That's when I bumped into something hanging there in the dark, something hanging from the winch. I walked out the back door of the barn and bumped into the nigger hanging there from the winch, his legs gone to the knee. Crows flew up, then settled back down on him. Their wings flapping sounded like fire, like the tongues of fire over the Apostles' heads. I stood there in the dark and thought: *Holy Ghost.*

Those birds had eaten out the nigger's eyes—his bodily eyes—and they'd eaten his lips.

I looked at the nigger hanging there. I couldn't move. I watched the birds cover him. Those crows. They were perched on his shoulders, perched on his head. Others were hovering. I could hear them in the dark. The dream I can't stop having is full of them: crows all over the nigger—Geronimo—more crows than I've ever seen fill the sky. My dream is filled with those birds, and the rustle of fire.

That night, too, there were the flies buzzing. Or maybe there weren't; maybe it was just that haywire sound in my ears. But I think I did see them. It looked like the nigger's hair was flying right off him, but I think it might have been flies.

The sound—the sound the flies were making—was the worst sound yet, worse than the sound of crows, but the smell was worse than that.

When I realized what it was that was hanging there, that it was the nigger—my Geronimo—when I saw the crows on him and heard the flies and felt those flies on my face, part of me went over by the pole fence and part of me went over by the river, to the elm tree above the pig pen. When I realized what I'd bumped into, I wasn't just standing there under the winch and our barn's rose window anymore. It was like I'd died and was on my way to heaven, only it wasn't heaven where I got. It was the feeling of getting to heaven, though, like when the swing started going over onto itself, that feeling that I wasn't in my skin anymore, of getting out of my skin, out of my circumstances, one step shy of flight.

That's when I went for the saddle room. I went straight to that room, made a beeline for it as soon as I was myself again, when I could walk and think. I got the key from the secret place by the red radio. I unlocked the door and opened it. I went right in, right to that secret drawer. It was locked so I took down the twelve-gauge that was hanging below the .25-20, leaving just the halo of the twelve-gauge on the wall. I blew a hole in the drawer, buckshot spraying every which way. Then I reached in there and got that secret envelope and opened it. After all those years, this is what I found:

There were five photographs of a woman taking off her clothes; in the first photograph, she had on her coat and her hat and her high heels. In the second photograph, she had a dress on and the high heels. In the third, she just had her slip on and the high heels. In the fourth photograph, she just had her bra on and her panties on. Her nylons hooked to that part that holds them up. In the fifth photograph, she was naked.

There was a coupon torn from a magazine to send away for a Spanish fly. *Drives the female wild,* it said on the coupon.

There was a picture of naked men, seven of them, standing on a lava rock by a lake, arm in arm, smiling. I think one of them was my father and the rest were his six brothers.

There was a photograph of four men in uniform. One of them was my father during the war, in Germany. The men in uniform were with a fifth man dressed up like a Negro woman with black on his face, smoking a cigar. The other three men and my father were looking at the man dressed up like a Negro woman, laughing and drinking beer.

And there was a photograph of a nurse who looked like Esther Williams. She'd signed the photograph, *To Joe, Always My Love, All of It, Eva,* and then there was something written in German. At least it looked like German to me.

There was a Trojan—"a contraceptive," it said on the outside of the package.

There was some strange-looking paper money, none of it green.

There was the sheet music to the Perry Como song "Faraway Places."

There was a Holy Card with the Holy Eucharist on it that said that Joseph Robert Weber had received his First Holy Communion. Along with the Holy Card was a photograph of my father—he was just a kid—standing next to his mother. Grandma Ruth looked younger but just as fat. My father was wearing a suit. There was a German shepherd dog in the background in front of a house that needed paint. At the bottom of the photograph was written: *My First Holy Communion Day, 1925.*

There was another photograph of my father in a suit with wide lapels and baggy pants. He stood in front of that same house, still in need of paint. My father was older in that one. The German shepherd was older too. My father's hand was on the dog's head. *Me and Fritz on my Holy Confirmation Day, 1933,* was written under the photograph, and this was written there too: *My Holy Confirmation Name: John,* it said. That's what it said and I wondered if my father had chosen the same John as I had—the St. John who wrestled with the devil.

That was it, at least I thought that was it, and then I saw a piece of silky cloth, a pink color, that had dropped out. I picked it up. It was like an envelope. I opened it and pulled out three more photographs and a blue ribbon like the kind you can win at the Blackfoot State Fair.

The blue ribbon said *Best Butterfly Collection, St. Veronica's School, Eighth Grade.*

Two of the photographs were of my mother: one was of her with a different hairstyle. In that she was wearing a real short dress. She was pulling up that short skirt even higher. Under the photograph she had written, *Gosh! Yah! Boy! Mary.*

The second was a photograph of my father kissing my mother at their wedding.

The third was of my father, smiling proudly, holding a little baby in his arms. Holding me.

And then I heard something. I looked up and saw my father standing in the doorway. He said: "What the hell are you doing?"

I looked him in the eye. That was the hardest thing—

looking into my father's eyes as he stood there in the doorway. There wasn't any secret anymore and there weren't any rules anymore and I was looking into his eyes.

My father started walking toward me, like he always did, like he was the one who knew it all, and he repeated his question, *what the hell are you doing here?*

I hauled off and hit him as hard as I could with the back of my hand.

My father stepped back, dazed, and wiped the blood from his mouth. Then looked at the blood on his hand, as if he couldn't believe it was real.

"Don't hate me, Jake—I was drunk," my father said.

My father never called me *Jake,* or *Jacob,* or *Jacob Joseph,* or *John.* He never called me *son.* He called me *Jake* when he talked to other people, but to me it was just *do this* or *do that.*

"I hated you before you were drunk," I said, and then I called him that name, called him *motherfucker.* "Motherfucker," I said.

My father looked down at the floor, at all his pictures, at his ribbon, at his Trojan, at the Spanish fly coupon, at the man dressed up like a Negro woman, at the Holy Eucharist, at Eva, at *Gosh! Yah! Boy!*

His chest was rising up and going down fast, just the way it would before he explodes when he gets mad. I still had the gun, though I didn't know if it was loaded still. My father just stood there breathing hard and deep and looking at the floor.

Then my father kind of slumped down to his knees;

his head was only inches from the barrel of the twelve-gauge. He picked up his blue ribbon in his big hairy hand, then picked up the picture of him and his dog Fritz on that day in 1933 when his new name was John.

The picture of him naked with his six brothers was right by my foot. I kicked it over to him. He picked it up and looked at it.

My father sat back on his feet and looked up at me. Then he picked up another photograph. I knew which one it was and wished he wouldn't have picked that one up—the one of him holding his little baby. He brought the photograph up close to his face, as though he couldn't quite make it out. With his chest going up and down like that, my father started to cry. He heaved a big sigh and looked up the barrel of the gun at me. His eyes were looking at me but they weren't really; they were looking at something, for something, that wasn't there anymore.

"How did it all happen at Endicott's that night?" my father finally asked.

"You wanted a fair fight, like a man," I said. "And Endicott whipped you. You dropped your guard," I said.

"When did the nigger kill him, do you know?" my father asked.

"How do you know it was the nigger who killed him?" I asked.

"The sheriff told me," my father said. "At first they thought Endicott died of natural causes and that his dogs got to him after that. But then they picked up the nigger on the highway, walking down the middle of the highway, with hardly nothing on and Endicott's whistle around his neck and part of Endicott's scalp hanging from his belt."

"Those people just got a nose for trouble," I said. And then I said, "He saved your life."

"Who saved my life?"

"The nigger, Geronimo, saved your life."

"Geronimo?" my father said.

"That's his name, the nigger's name," I said.

"Saved my life?" my father said.

"He shot Endicott with his bow and arrow. Endicott was going for his dogs to sic them on you and turn you into what they turned that woman Sugar Babe into, but Geronimo stopped him, shot him in the eye. I saw it all," I said.

The sky started to come in the room then, black sky, no stars.

"How'd Endicott get back in the house then?" my father said.

"We put him in there, and then covered our tracks. Then we covered yours."

"And both of you carried me back here?" my father said.

"Yes," I said. "In Old Glory. But I didn't make it all the way."

I heard the screen door slam.

"Mom found us both lying there by the back door

in the rain wrapped up in the flag," my father told me. "She said it was a miracle." He looked at the ground and shook his head. "Why?" he said.

"Why what?" I said.

"Why did he do it, the nigger—"

"Geronimo," I said.

"—Geronimo," my father said. "Why did he do it?"

"She was his mother," I said. "Sugar Babe was his mother."

It got real quiet in the saddle room then, my father's chest rising up and going down. "We'll have to tell the sheriff," he finally said.

"Why?" I said.

"Because maybe we can get Geronimo off—for saving my life."

"You don't know?" I said.

"Know what?" my father said.

I hung the twelve-gauge back up on the wall, inside its halo.

I stepped aside, holding the door open for my father. I let him walk through the back door of the barn and into the navy-blue night. I let my father step right into the nigger. I let him bump into him just the way I did.

I'd taken the flashlight from its halo on the wall, and when my father bumped into the nigger hanging there from the winch, I shined the light into my father's face. Then I shined it into the nigger's.

My father's face was against the nigger's crotch. My father tried to get his balance. He had to touch the nigger with his hands to get his balance back. My father tried not to touch the nigger, but he had to. It was either that or fall.

And then my father looked up to see just what it was he'd bumped into. I helped him by shining the flashlight his way.

It was more horrible than even I thought it was with the flashlight on like that. Even the smell was worse when you could see it.

I felt good that it was horrible, then. For my father's sake.

I watched my father start to make funny noises: grunts and sighs and little-girl screams. I watched him jump away like he was on a pogo stick. I watched him fall down, away from the nigger. My father was wiping his hands, trying to get that nigger's blood off. I watched him howl and start crying again, this time loud with big sobs.

"I didn't know! I didn't know! God forgive me, I didn't know!" my father was crying.

After a while my father got quiet again. He got up off his knees. Then he bent over and puked—three times. He wiped his mouth on his shirt sleeve and stood up as straight as he could manage. He walked over to me, but I wasn't afraid. He couldn't hurt me anymore.

But he did. My father hurt me again.

My father just walked over and put his arms around me, just walked up to me—no problem—after all those years and grabbed on to my neck and hugged me, hugged me because he needed it. Maybe because he thought I needed it too.

But I didn't hug him back. Touching him was like him touching the nigger. I only held on to keep my balance.

I was still holding the door open, and my father was still holding on to me and crying when I realized my mother was standing there in the doorway. She was a mess. Her hair was sticking up all over the place; her dress was torn. She had let herself go, like the time when the chinook first hit us. It was dark but I could see how her eye was, and my mother looked at me like she knew I was fed up with making things nice when things weren't nice. And I knew she was fed up too.

My mother was holding a large crucifix and Old Glory and a can of gasoline.

My father looked at her, then at me. There we were: one man's family.

My mother handed me and my father shovels, and we dug the nigger's grave right there in the corral. The digging wasn't tough; the ground was soft below the manure. We were all quiet. The sky was everywhere. The sky went deeper and deeper the more we dug. My father started crying and had to stop shoveling twice.

Both times he leaned against the shovel and said what a fool he had been. I still didn't say anything, and neither did my mother.

Then my mother went and got the twelve-gauge. She stood close and aimed at the lariat hanging from the winch and pulled the trigger. The crows flew off the nigger in an explosion of black wings. The sound of that shot was like the screen door slamming. The nigger fell down to the ground onto Old Glory with a sound like when you throw a sack of rotten spuds out to pigs. We dragged the Old Glory bundle to the grave and dropped it in, then covered it up with dirt. We threw dirt and manure, one shovelful at a time, on top of Old Glory, on top of the nigger, on top of Geronimo, and when we were done, my mother put the crucifix on the grave.

I went to the river and sat down by the edge. I took my boots off and my socks off and stuffed my socks in my boots and rolled up my pants legs. I waded across the shallow part to the small island of brambles and scrub elms and went around behind where no one could see me. I took off my shirt and my Levi's and my shorts and stuffed my shorts in my pants. Then I jumped in the river, in the deep part, still only about four feet deep. I swam around naked, my first time swimming naked like that. Before, I'd always worn my shorts. This was my first time standing naked with sky all around. I washed out my Levi's and my shirt and shorts and wrung them out. I put them back on wet and when I came back around from back there where no one could see me, I saw my mother standing in the river, water up to her knees. The skirt of her red housedress floated in a circle around her. She put her face down close to the water and cupped the water up to her face and hair. She splashed herself over and over again, then straightened up and shook her hair out, shaking her head from side to side fast with her eyes closed, water spraying from her hair.

My mother stood there for a while, like she was trying to decide what to do, all the while looking at her hands. Then she made the sign of the cross with her right hand, her left hand pulling her hair back from her face. I knew she did that because she didn't know what else to do. She turned and waded up to the bank and walked without turning to look at my father. He was kneeling there by the river, over by the elm tree by the pig pen. He just knelt there rubbing his hands together in the water and looking at things strange, as if he had never seen the world before.

My mother knelt down by the grave to pray to God and the Virgin Mary, and my father—when he saw that she was kneeling down by the grave—came over and knelt down beside her. My mother's eye told me to kneel down at the grave too.

But I didn't.

Instead, I sang the *heya, heya, Geronimo* song and danced around and let myself go like a wild animal. I sang the *heya, heya, Sugar Babe* song too. The crows heard my song, and the pigeons in the barn heard, and the hawks. The river heard and so did the trees along the river. I don't know if God heard my song, but the rest of them heard and that was enough.

I danced and sang and I watched my mother and my father. They didn't act like it was unusual that I was dancing. They acted like I was doing something ordinary, which surprised me a little, but then I wasn't dancing for them to see. I didn't care what they thought. I thought of digging up Old Glory, of crawling inside that grave my father and I had dug. I would have liked to have slept and dreamed dreams with Geronimo. But he was already too far away.

What I didn't know then as I danced, watching my mother and watching my father, was how many times, uncountable times, I would live through all of this again: the chinook, the *heya, heya, Geronimo* and *heya, heya, Sugar Babe* songs, yellow stains and red flags, butterflies and dice, Black Velvet and the river, one thing always leading to another forevermore.

My mother poured gasoline onto the spot where the nigger had fallen onto Old Glory. She lit a match and looked at it, both eyes perfectly focused on the flame. Then she tossed the match onto the spot. Flames from that single flame blew up high with a sound, huge and forevermore like hell. The sound the barn made when the flames got to it, after my mother had sprinkled gasoline all around, was like the sound she made shaking her hair out in the river.

The shingles were on fire, the floorboards were, even the strands of light coming down from the holes in the roof in the loft were aflame. The red radio was burning, the bag balm, and so were the milk strainers. The saddle room was on fire.

I managed to get two of those photographs out of the saddle room before the barn blew altogether. It was a close one, but I got the two I wanted. When I walked past the toolshed, the toolshed burst into flames too. It was like war, like a bomb bursting in air, like God—too bright.

The Oldsmobile was parked away from the house, its engine running. My father was standing around like he was drunk again on Black Velvet. He walked to the middle of the yard, watching things the way he had been watching at the river. He watched my mother walk out of the house with two big suitcases I had never seen before. She was wearing her hat, the one she didn't wear that much anymore, the one with the pheasant feather in it. Her hair was still a mess, but she had her high heels on, but no lipstick and no nylons either. She set the suitcases down and closed the screen door tight, snugged it back into home. By the time she got to the Oldsmobile, the house blew too. She didn't even flinch, like one thing had just led to another in a way she knew it would all along. I thought of the things in our house that were burning: the kitchen table, the beds, my father's chair, the coffee table, the doily curtains, the medicine-cabinet mirror, the wallpaper in the hallway, my confirmation diploma, the guardian-angel picture with the kids. My mother put the suitcases in the trunk of the Oldsmobile and got in on the driver's side, closing the door behind her.

My father didn't budge; he just kept standing there in the middle of the yard, fire all around: big, greedy flames going lickety-split, the whole shebang on fire. The color was like a sunset right there in front of you all the time. My father looked young, like he had when he was in the army. He looked scared. I walked over to him and gave him one of the photographs, the one of him kissing my mother at their wedding, but I kept the other one—my favorite. I put that one in my shirt pocket.

My father stared at the photograph for some time, then at the fire; flames everywhere grew higher. My mother had the Oldsmobile running in neutral.

The sun began to rise.

I didn't say good-bye to anything when I left. I didn't cry. The sky was a color I had never seen before and the fire was making me sweat even though I was already way down the road past the last red flag before the house.

I didn't look back. I just walked out of the yard and onto the road and headed west because I didn't want to see the river, or Harold P. Endicott's house, or where his flag used to snap in the sky. I didn't want to see that woman Sugar Babe's lean-to, the one she'd shared with the nigger, or the trees along the river. I didn't want to see the place up there in the stand of twenty-two cottonwood trees where my swing used to be.

I could still feel the heat on my back by the second flag. And as that fire burned, the wind was at my back, blowing from that direction it never blew from, but the once.

The Oldsmobile pulled up next to me on the gravel road. My mother was driving and my father was beside her. I kept on walking and my mother kept driving slow, her eyes on the road, my eyes on the road, her left eye gone that way it gets, not that I looked to see.

My mother turned on the radio, to the rock-and-roll station. It was my favorite song playing: "Walk, Don't Run," by the Ventures.

I thought about what was lying under that cross, under the manure, wrapped in Old Glory. I wondered if that crucifix was on fire yet, and I wondered if Geronimo was in heaven, or if that, too, was just another illusion. *Everything,* Mr. Energy had said, *everything is an illusion.*

I wondered what the davenport looked like burning, what the hallway looked like burning, and the confirmation certificate, and the picture of the guardian angel. I wondered if the butterflies and the dice burned off the wallpaper first.

My father opened the car door and put his hand out to me. I walked ahead for a while before I took it and got in the Oldsmobile with them. My mother drove off with us in the car like that, her looking that way in her hat with the pheasant feather, hair sticking out all over, my father in the middle, blood still on his face, staring at me like he had never set eyes on me before; my mother driving and trying to light a Viceroy, me by the window, riding shotgun with "Walk, Don't Run" turned up high.

I rolled down the window and rested my arm on the side of the car. I could see myself in the rearview mirror and I watched myself for a while. Then I turned the mirror so I could see what was burning up behind me.

I took a long look back.

Framed that way in the mirror, it looked like the photograph of the Industrial Revolution from that book Mr. Hoffman gave me: all that smoke and fire going up into the Pittsburgh, Pennsylvania sky.

For a second I wondered if what I could see back there behind the Oldsmobile could be reflected ahead, so that what was happening back there looked like it was happening up front too. I tried to adjust the mirror to see if I could do that—see forward by reflecting what was back—but it didn't quite work. When we got to the red flag on the plateau, I stopped looking into the mirror. I stuck my head out the window and turned around.

The flames were licking up high and wild in the middle of that flat cookie sheet, and in the dawn's early light, you could see the moon hanging up there dim in the blue infinity, and the sun, a much larger flame, rising in the eastern sky.